GARY SOTO

PUPPY LOVE

Clarion Books

An Imprint of HarperCollinsPublishers

Clarion Books is an imprint of HarperCollins Publishers.

Puppy Love
Copyright © 2023 by Gary Soto
All rights reserved. Printed in the United States of America.
No part of this book may be used or reproduced in any manner whatsoever
without written permission except in the case of brief quotations
embodied in critical articles and reviews.
For information address HarperCollins Children's Books,
a division of HarperCollins Publishers, 195 Broadway, New York, NY 10007.
www.harpercollinschildrens.com

Library of Congress Control Number: 2023930319
ISBN 978-0-06-326778-7

Typography by Sarah Nichole Kaufman
23 24 25 26 27 LBC 5 4 3 2 1

First Edition

For Gina Tranisi

1

JORDAN SAT on a sheet of discarded cardboard, his eyes following the wavering light on the water of the canal that ran through the city. He was not happy with himself. He dwelled on the humiliation of his failure, witnessed not only by family, classmates, and school boosters, but also by Sierra Mendez, a girl he liked. She was pretty but also nice, real nice. This was what he liked best about her.

Jordan replayed the scene. She had been seated among friends near the top of the bleachers, rooting for the school team, the Patriots. She would have seen him at his most inept, her mouth open in utter shock. How had he missed that shot, an easy layup that would have put his team up by a point? The basketball had circled the rim, as if debating whether to go in.

But it didn't.

It swirled teasingly, spanked the backboard, then swirled one more time before falling to the side like a rock to the hardwood court. An opposing player grabbed the ball, hugging it to his chest as if to say *It's mine, all mine.* The spectators, who had been mostly on their feet during the last seconds of a close game, let out a communal "Aaah . . ."

In that instant, Jordan imagined Sierra, head lowered and biting a knuckle. Her eyes, squeezed closed, would have shown disappointment when they opened. With all the noisy spectators in the bleachers, her sigh would not have been heard.

"How could you," Jordan imagined her saying, "how could you miss such an easy shot?" But, to be honest, Jordan didn't know if Sierra was even aware of his existence. Unless she'd turned to a friend and asked, "Who's that player who missed the basket?"

Jordan Mendoza!

After the miss, when he had glanced up at the bleachers, he had spotted his friend Antonio on his phone. Had he been posting to the world about Jordan's failure? And what about Jordan's teammates? Had they sympathized with him? A glance at the bench said otherwise. They had been on their feet, shouting in shock, anger, and frustration—shouting with actual personal dislike for him, Jordan Mendoza, age thirteen.

The Patriots' best player, Ryan Greene, lanky and tall, had remained standing under the basket, confused. It was obvious what he was thinking—*How could Jordan's layup not go in?*

In the most important game of his life, Jordan Mendoza had wimped out.

That had been Thursday afternoon. Now on an autumn Saturday, Jordan sat alone on the sandy canal bank. Even the usually attentive pigeons had winged away when he showed up. To comfort himself, he recalled his parents' reactions. His father had squeezed his shoulder and murmured, "It's OK, *mi'jo*." His mother had said, "At least you tried."

At least you tried?

What comfort was that? He felt horrible and would continue to feel horrible for rest of his life—or at least until the end of seventh grade. Jordan crumpled a leaf in his left hand, which hurt. It hurt because, seconds after the buzzer had sounded, he had punched a concrete wall, tearing a few patches of skin off his knuckles.

On Friday—the day after the debacle—his usually friendly classmates had avoided him. Most walked away from him, but Ryan, the star who had piled up sixteen of their team's thirty-seven points, bumped him in the hallway.

"Hey!" Jordan shouted.

But Ryan hadn't looked back. Instead, he'd swaggered away and raised a finger in the air.

"Dang," Jordan muttered to himself. If he had made the

basket, his team would have advanced to the first round of the all-city finals. Now there was no afternoon practice, no huddling together on the gym court, no expectations of glory, *nada* but silence and the image of Ryan's finger in the air.

Worse, Antonio had sent him a three-second clip, with the message: "Bro, this is what's out there." Jordan watched it once, then immediately deleted it. Not only had he missed the layup, but he'd looked clumsy as he leapt into the air—with his tongue sticking out, a fat thing that made him look ugly.

Why had he even gone out for the basketball team? True, he was tall for his age, but height didn't guarantee success on the court. He could have joined the chess club and spent his lunchtime with nerds. *Nerds*, he'd realized, after one had helped him on an algebra assignment, *were good people.*

Jordan watched the flickering shine on the canal. The moving water flowed swiftly and abundantly from the Sierra Nevada mountains, east of town. He had swum in it with Antonio—swum and ridden a tractor inner tube down the canal until they were nearly in the countryside. They would have ridden the current until it ended in a dribble of muddy water, except that a county sheriff in a dusty cruiser ordered them out.

"Do you know how dangerous the canal is?" the sheriff

scolded. "Boy a little younger than you drowned here last month!"

That had been last summer, when life was like the canal: sunny on the surface and flowing with hardly a ripple. Now Jordan sat on the bank, cradling his hurt hand. He recalled his late grandmother. She believed that time healed even the worst in life. But did it? He didn't like the idea that the spectators—his mom and dad included—had captured him on their phones. Those images were forever, unless you lost your phone or upgraded and got a new one.

"Ah," he whispered under his breath. "I wish I could start seventh grade over." He was pulling fair-to-good grades and was sort of popular, sort of athletic, and sort of responsible when it came to volunteer service. If only it was the start of the school year, not a cold November day. Then he wouldn't even be thinking about a basketball game.

Jordan sighed, then placed the thicker end of a blade of grass in his mouth. He was absently observing the canal's flow again when he spotted an object in the water—a brown thing that, for a second, resembled a sports cap and then, as it got closer, a shoe.

"What the heck," he murmured. He stood up, grains of sand falling from his pants.

The shoe blinked at him as it passed, paws paddling for its life.

A puppy!

Jordan spat out the blade of grass and raced to the water's edge, his shoes sinking into the mud. He hurried along the bank, brushing aside the branches of willows and leaping over a fallen chain-link fence. He jumped over some car parts, a shopping cart, a mini-refrigerator, two rusty bicycles. He wasn't about to let that puppy drown.

The puppy churned its paws to keep afloat. Its small head disappeared under the surface, then reappeared. The current was pulling it away from the bank.

Jordan had no choice. He stepped into the water and waded in waist-deep, hugging himself from the sudden cold. Then he plunged in, clothes and all. The icy chill stunned his heart but he swam after the puppy, then rode the current around a bend. He had taken swimming lessons since third grade and mastered every stroke. His mom called him a dolphin, but his dad disagreed. "Jordan," he said, "is more like a killer shark."

Now, with his head just above the surface, Jordan looked to his right. He noticed two younger boys on the bank with sticks in their hands—a sword fight, no doubt. They eyed him, mouths open, swords down. One pointed while the other shouted, "Why are you in there?"

Why am I in here? A good question, but how could he begin to explain through chattering teeth?

Jordan swept out of their view as the current picked up speed. He still trailed the puppy by several yards but was gaining on it. His breaststroke pulled him closer until he was right behind it. He tried twice before successfully grasping the puppy's scruff. He drew the small body toward his chest. Even wet, the puppy weighed almost nothing.

Legs kicking, Jordan swam toward the grassy bank, hugging his precious cargo with one arm. When his shoes touched bottom, he rose like a monster from the canal. His clothes shed sheets of water and slimy weeds. His teeth were chattering, his arms pimpled from the cold.

The puppy sneezed, then Jordan sneezed. His water-logged phone beeped once, then stopped. He plucked the phone from his back pocket. Another classmate had sent him the image of his failed attempt at an easy layup.

Who cares?

He hugged the puppy and began to run home, dripping water.

2

THE PUPPY was sleeping on an old, paint-stained sweatshirt near the television.

"Tell me again," Jordan's father asked from his recliner, pressing the mute button on the remote. The TV was on but the football match—the *Chivas* against a team from South America—was a matter of small importance, a noise to fill the living room.

Jordan sneezed twice. Startled, the pup looked up and around. It licked its paw for a few seconds, then lowered its head again.

"Sorry, Dad." Jordan blew his nose.

"It must have been cold," Mr. Mendoza remarked with sympathy.

"Yeah, it was." Jordan told him again how he had gone alone to the canal to nurse his pain.

"Son, that's not pain—players miss baskets all the time."

"Not when someone special is looking."

Jordan's father let this sentence ricochet inside his head for a few moments before asking, "What's her name?"

"How do you know it's a girl?"

"Because I was a boy once."

Dad was once a boy?

Jordan's dad fingered the remote and the television went black. "And I had an experience kind of like yours— that's why." He pushed a lever on his recliner and sat up straight. To Jordan, he resembled the Pope, seated in a magisterial chair with a high back. "See, when I was just a couple years older than you are now," he began.

Mr. Mendoza's experience had involved junior varsity football. He, a third-string running back, had fumbled the ball on the two-yard line, fumbled when a girl he liked was watching. He ran a hand over his mouth after he told Jordan about it, as if wiping away some unpleasant truth.

"I liked her a lot," he reminisced. "She was a cheerleader, beautiful, smart, kind . . ." His dreamy description of her trailed off.

"What do you mean by a lot?" Jordan asked.

"The very reason why you're here," his dad said mysteriously. He munched on his lower lip, then revealed, "I'm talking about your mother."

Mom? Mom was a cheerleader?

"I fumbled the football while Mom was doing her cheerleader thing." He slapped the arms of his recliner. "I could've been the star of the game. But clumsy me, I had to fumble it."

"Was your team good?"

"We stunk. Went 2–7 that year."

Jordan noticed that the puppy had woken up and was licking its front paws again. His mom had never mentioned that she was a cheerleader. She was super nice, but it was hard for him to imagine her as popular. And why would a cheerleader pair up with a player who had fumbled the ball?

"Dad?" Jordan asked.

"What?"

"Does it run in the family?"

"Does what run in the family?"

"That we mess up when the girls we like are watching us."

Jordan pictured Sierra in the bleachers, her eyes downcast from embarrassment.

His dad cracked a knuckle and pondered the question, forehead pleated with wrinkles. From his papal throne, he answered, "I think so."

Jordan's mother came into the living room then, rattling a box like a maraca. She looked from husband to son and then back to husband.

"I heard you two. I was no cheerleader—I was a booster."

"A booster?" Mr. Mendoza remarked loudly. "Is that what you were?" He pounded the arm of his recliner. "And to think that all these years I thought you were a cheerleader."

"Wrong, Mr. Smarty Pants. I was a booster."

She educated Jordan on the difference: cheerleaders were those lithe types usually thrown into the air and caught, while boosters were girls—and guys—who beat pom-poms together and rallied their team to victory. Boosters never, ever kicked their legs skyward. And they weren't as popular as cheerleaders among the jocks.

Jordan's father opened his mouth, ready to correct his wife, but wisely said nothing. He breathed in, breathed out, then asked, "What do you got there?"

Jordan's mom rattled the box. "Cat food. Do you think the puppy will like cat food?"

The cat nibbles were old, the favorite of their late cat, Mercury. Mercury had died a year ago and was buried in the yard. A circle of clamshells marked his grave.

"Nah, Mom," said Jordan, "I think we need puppy food."

When Jordan had returned home, wet and slimy with canal water, Mrs. Mendoza had screamed in surprise. She was a homemaker, used to defending what Jordan's father called "the fort," but in this case she couldn't be sure exactly what threat she was facing. Jordan had removed his shoes and his hoodie and T-shirt. He was bare-chested in the cold November air, with a brownish mop-like thing in the crook of his arm.

But after recognizing the urgency of the situation, his

mother had immediately gone into action. She toweled the puppy dry and cleaned the corners of its eyes. Then she opened a can of evaporated milk and shook a few drops onto her fingers and into its mouth.

That had been earlier in the day. Now it was dark out and the puppy was the center of attention.

"How old do you think he is?" Jordan asked.

"A month old," his mother guessed.

"Could grow up to be big," Mr. Mendoza offered. "We could use a guard dog."

"Dad," Jordan said, "you know that's not true. We live in a safe area." Then he turned to his mother. "Mom, how did you feel when Dad fumbled the ball?"

Mrs. Mendoza's face softened as she tried her best to recall the occasion. After a moment, she said honestly, "I wasn't looking."

"Really? You never told me that before." Jordan's dad slapped his thighs. "After all these years you tell me you didn't see my mess-up?"

Jordan dropped to his knees and stroked the puppy's head. Then his father got out of his recliner and joined them.

Mercury must have been turning in his grave.

A dog eating my nibbles?

3

JORDAN WOKE UP before dawn, startled. He leapt from the bed, chest heaving as if he had just been chased through a nightmare. He looked wildly around his bedroom, uncertain of where he was.

"There's another one," he whispered to himself.

As his breathing calmed, Jordan stepped into a fresh pair of jeans, then wrestled a hoodie over his head. He skipped his socks and hurried to the living room, where he knelt and petted the puppy. He opened an eye and nudged Jordan's knuckle with a wet nose. A wet nose, Jordan knew, suggested that the puppy wasn't sick. How he had survived the ride down the icy cold canal was a mystery.

In the kitchen, Jordan gazed at the clock on the microwave oven: 5:40. He grabbed a banana and slipped noiselessly out the back to avoid waking his parents. The door made a *click* as it closed, then he was alone in the near dark.

He fitted his feet into his soggy sneakers and stepped off the back porch. He got his bike from the garage, mounted it in the driveway, and popped a wheelie as he sped away. With only the predawn light to guide him—and the occasional passing car—he pedaled down dim streets. When he spotted a police cruiser, he skidded to a halt and lurked behind a tree. How could he explain to a cop his need to get somewhere quick in the middle of the night, that somewhere being the canal?

After the cruiser passed, Jordan continued, his legs burning from exertion. By the time he arrived at the canal, the sun was edging up and over the roofs of homes. A few roosters were crowing. Somewhere not far off a leaf blower was starting up.

He threw his bike into some bushes and trudged over the loose sand toward the bank of the canal. The water was murky, not yet lit by sunlight, not yet mirroring the clouds above.

He's got to have a brother—or a sister, Jordan told himself. He looked upstream, from where the puppy had come, paddling for dear life.

Jordan walked along the bank, dodging debris and garbage, pushing against branches that snapped back after his passing. He stepped into a puddle, which left his shoes even colder than before. His nose began to run.

Eventually he came upon a homeless man in a sleeping bag and paused to stare. The man stared back, eyes dark as ash. Neither of them said a word, even after Jordan handed the man his banana, offering it like a baton. The homeless man examined this unexpected gift, then placed it at his side.

"Wish I had more," Jordan caught himself saying.

The man shrugged.

Jordan observed the contents of a plastic bottle next to the sleeping bag—from the look of it, the man was drinking right from the canal. He felt sad knowing this.

Jordan continued on his trek, sunlight now touching the surface of the water. He walked nearly a mile, scanning left and right. He was convinced that his puppy had a brother or a sister. Mother dogs never gave birth to only one pup.

Then Jordan saw a hint of movement on the bank. As he approached, he could see two puppies, one squirming and alive and the other quiet, its eyes closed. He stood still for a few seconds, trying to absorb the moment.

"I'm so sorry," Jordan murmured. He approached the pups and knelt before them. He picked up the live puppy and raised it to eye level—it was a girl. He fit her into the pocket of his hoodie. The other he cupped in his hands and took to higher ground. There, Jordan glanced around for something to use as a shovel.

"I'm sorry," Jordan said again. He had buried his cat Mercury, but that rascal had enjoyed a long life of prancing around the neighborhood. This puppy had lived only weeks, maybe a month, and for all Jordan knew it had survived without comfort and love. Where the puppies had come from—what yard, what house—he couldn't say. But he was sure that they had been heartlessly abandoned. How could someone throw away innocent puppies like trash?

Jordan broke a bottle on a rock and used the sharp end to dig a grave. He placed the dead puppy there, said a prayer, then smoothed dirt over it. Because it was November, there were no flowers. He snapped a branch from a bush and stuck it in the ground at the head of the grave. This was the best he could offer.

Jordan stood up, said one more prayer, and made his way back to his bike. He hurried home with the puppy bouncing in the pouch of his hoodie as if he were a kangaroo mother. He had another puppy to keep alive!

Jordan and his parents stood over the new arrival, who immediately nestled next to her brother. None of them said a word and nobody moved. They were quiet for what seemed like a long time.

"Son," Mrs. Mendoza began.

Jordan looked at his mom.

"We were worried about you."

Jordan felt like crying.

"*But mi'jo*, you did good." Mr. Mendoza squeezed Jordan's shoulder, then glanced up at the kitchen clock: 7:00.

He grimaced at his phone. "Another day on the planet—got to go. Someone's shower won't turn off." He squeezed Jordan's shoulder again, then exited by the back door, only to return a moment later to grab his hat from its hook. "Jordan," he repeated, "you did good."

Jordan's mother dotted warm milk onto the end of her finger and offered it to the new arrival.

"Poor little thing," she cooed. "Without a mom."

"Or a dad," Jordan added.

"That's right." She stroked the brownish fur of the new puppy. "We need to come up with names for them."

Jordan nodded and went into the kitchen to make himself a quesadilla. He ate leaning against the sink while his mind rumbled with potential names.

4

ON MONDAY MORNING, the school was bustling with kids pushing each other along a narrow foyer, where a large portrait of the school's namesake glared down on them. *Had George Washington ever been a teenager?* Jordan wondered. The students surged through the double doors without a thought for the first president. He was a Founding Father, but he didn't get much consideration—except on the occasions when someone adorned his nose with a wad of gum. That gum often stayed in place for days before being yanked off by a janitor.

Now Jordan squeezed through the horde of students, happily so, because he figured that his inconspicuousness kept his classmates from asking, "Hey, bro, how come you missed that layup?"

He needed to be alone. He wanted nothing more than to post himself behind the school's seldom-used brick barbecue. There he would quietly devour a packet of white powdery donuts, enough nutrition to get him through the first two periods, algebra and social studies. But Jordan didn't reach his hiding place.

"Hey," a voice called.

Jordan had responded to this "hey" hundreds of times. But today he kept going. It took a loud "Hey, bro, I got to talk to you" to make him stop. Wheeling around, he faced his friend Antonio.

"About what?" Jordan asked.

"Hope you ain't feeling bad."

"Actually, I am," Jordan said. "Let me suffer quietly."

"Sorry, bro." Antonio pulled a packet of donuts from his hoodie pocket—glazed ones that shone as if they were sweating. He offered one to Jordan.

"Nah, I'm good."

Antonio hesitated, then said, "Bro, it's, like, every-where."

Everywhere.

"Even your girlfriend—"

"I don't have a girlfriend!" Jordan looked down, wondering if he could get through his first two classes without a bite of something sweet. He pulled out his own donuts and squinted at them.

"That's right," Antonio agreed. "She ain't your girl-friend, *yet.*"

Jordan brooded. He was still hurting from his moment of disgrace. He had come to the barbecue stand to hide. And now this.

"Man, I like school," said Antonio, changing the sub-ject.

"You like school?" Jordan remarked. "Really?"

"Yeah, really," he mumbled through a second donut. He wolfed it down in three bites, cleared his throat, then croaked, "There's so much drama—good drama. Like Sierra—she's nice, if you know her like I know her. She asked me to ask you 'bout how you feel."

Jordan blinked, unsure how to respond. "And what did you say?"

"I told her you're feeling hecka bad about missing that basket."

Was that a good answer? Jordan wondered. Then he asked, "Did she really say that or are you making it up? Be honest." Antonio was a real friend but the dude could tease.

"Nah, bro, I'm serious here."

For a few seconds, Jordan pictured himself sitting on a bench, far away from school. Sierra sat beside him, comforting him with her beautiful voice. "It doesn't matter that you missed the layup," she said. "I know you're really good at basketball—I do, honestly."

Jordan smiled to himself.

"What you smilin' about?" Antonio asked.

"I was just thinking."

"THINKING! Like, we're in seventh grade. We ain't supposed to be thinking. Nah, we're all about enjoying." He considered the donut in his hands. "Like what we eat," he added, pausing to look down at his stylish shoes, "and what we wear!" Then he asked why Jordan wasn't answering his phone.

"Like I told you, man," Jordan explained, "it got wet when I jumped in the canal. It's ruined."

"Bro, I don't know 'bout that story," said Antonio suspiciously. "Did you really jump into the canal to save a dog?"

"It's the truth, and there's more to it." He told his friend how he had gone back to the canal that very morning and saved a second puppy.

"Really? And your parents didn't get mad?"

"Nah."

"You're lucky. My mom would've filled my ears with a lot of screaming."

Someone shouted Antonio's name, then bellowed, "Hey, *Menso!*"

"I gotta go. Some fool's calling me." Antonio pushed his hands skyward, as if shooting a three-pointer. "Hey," he said, "after school—you, me."

Jordan massaged the knuckles of his left hand, being careful to avoid the new scabs. "Yeah, that's right," he replied. "The mall."

Antonio skipped backward, then hurried away, pulling up his pants with one hand and waving at the boy who had called to him.

5

AFTER SCHOOL, Jordan and Antonio strolled the indoor mall, stopping for free samples from Here's the Scoop.

The two boys paused in front of a tattoo and piercing shop. "When will your mom let you get your ears done?" Antonio asked.

"Like never," Jordan answered.

"My mom says next year." Antonio balled up the paper cup—the ice cream was history—then tossed it into a cement wastebasket. "Dang," he shouted, "I should join the basketball team!"

The store window was too dark to see through, but heavy metal music leaked from inside. It sounded to Jordan like music Darth Vader could dance to.

"You wanna go in?" Antonio dared. "Just to ask how much it costs?"

"You mean, ear piercing?"

Antonio nodded.

They entered, both slightly uneasy. The place was creepy and moist—like Darth Vader breathing into a toilet roll.

A thin man sitting behind a glass counter looked up, but said nothing. He was inked all the way to his throat and a ring with a chrome ball was attached to his nose. His ponytail was long enough to drape over one shoulder and hang down onto his chest. He put down his phone.

"Can I help you?" he asked, revealing another chrome ball on his tongue. He swished his ponytail across his other shoulder.

Antonio stepped forward. "Does it hurt?" he asked loudly.

"Does what hurt?" the man replied. "You mean getting a tattoo?"

"No," Jordan said, "piercing."

"Both," Antonio corrected him.

Jordan turned to Antonio and mouthed silently, *Both?*

The man stood up, scooting his chair behind him. He turned down the music, each finger gleaming darkly with rings.

"Well, it depends," he answered. "Like a belly ring—"

"No," Antonio interrupted, "I meant ear piercing."

"We're an artist studio," the man said. "We don't do ears. Our tattoos are very highly rated on Yelp."

The boys looked at each other but said nothing.

"Look," the man continued, "you're in, what, sixth grade?"

"Sixth grade!" roared Antonio. "We flunked sixth

grade," he joked, "now we're in seventh. Thirteen!"

"Sorry," said the man politely. "It's hard to judge ages, you know."

"And my bro here," said Antonio, pointing a hitchhiker's thumb at Jordan, "he's the captain of the basketball team."

"Shut up!" scolded Jordan. Then, turning to the tattooed man, he explained, "I play ball, but I'm not the captain."

The man suggested that they visit a jeweler for ear piercing. "But you'll need one of your parents there," he added, looking from Antonio to Jordan and back to Antonio. "As for tattoos—yeah, they can hurt. You cry a little and scream a little and even bleed a little."

"Bleed?" said Antonio. "We bleed all the time. Like last week I got my *nalgas* whipped."

"Tony, you lie," Jordan said, slightly embarrassed by his boisterous friend.

"You know I did," insisted Antonio. "The girl was tough."

The man smiled and said that he had to get back to work. He picked up a sheaf of papers from the counter.

As soon as the boys left the shop, they started talking about how the place seemed icky.

"For all we know," Jordan said, "the germs could be seeping into our skin right now."

"I got the answer to that," Antonio offered, producing a small bottle of hand sanitizer from his pocket. It was nearly empty, and the liquid came out in farting sounds.

"Was that you?" Jordan asked.

"You know it wasn't me," Antonio protested. "It was the bottle." Then he lifted a finger to his chin. "No," he went on, "wait a minute, it *was* me." He shrugged and laughed.

Thirteen was such a good age—Jordan hoped he never grew up.

The boys returned to the ice cream store to sample a different flavor.

"Weren't you just here?" the server asked.

"Indeed we were," Antonio said in an agreeable voice. "We're still deciding what to get for my birthday party. Like, everyone's gonna be invited."

Birthday party, Jordan thought. *Didn't it just pass?*

The woman behind the counter eyed them suspiciously. Still, she picked up a scoop, then dished out a new flavor: a combination of bubble gum and Oreo cookies.

A few steps out of the store, Antonio pointed. "Look."

"Look at what?" Jordan was licking melting ice cream from the side of his paper cup.

Antonio gestured with his chin in the direction of a boy and a girl about their age.

"Them?" asked a confused Jordan.

"My former girlfriend." Antonio sighed and brought

a spoonful of ice cream toward his mouth. "Guess she hooked up with some new fool."

"Man, you lie," Jordan said. "You have never had a girl-friend."

"And you have?"

"Yeah."

"Like who?"

"Like . . ." Jordan searched his memory. "Like Melissa Contreras."

"Melissa Contreras from third grade? Impossible."

"Why?"

"Because, dude, she was *my* girlfriend! That's why!" Antonio laughed and licked his fingers, starting with his thumb. Then he lowered his face to the cup and let his tongue wiggle against the last of the ice cream.

"But now I got someone I do like," Jordan said, becoming serious. "Sierra Mendez."

Antonio listened straight-faced to this news. Then he rumbled with laughter. "I thought it over. Ain't gonna happen."

Jordan scowled. Sierra was no laughing matter. "Why?"

"Why? You ask why?"

"Yeah, I'm asking why."

"Because, dude, she's in love with me!" He shot his paper cup at the wastebasket. And for the second time that afternoon, it went in.

6

JORDAN RETURNED HOME with chocolate stains near one corner of his mouth.

"Mom," he called from outside the back door. He wiped his shoes on the mat that read "Wipe Your Shoes." "Mom, you home?"

Except for the leaking faucet, a drip that plopped into a cereal bowl once every three seconds, the house was silent. In the living room, he found one of the puppies— the boy—tottering about. It reminded him of a windup toy ready to fall over.

"Hey, little dude!" Jordan dropped to his knees and felt the pup's snout—it was damp and cool. He beamed inwardly. He remembered all the times when he'd been down with a fever and his mom would feel his nose—hot he stayed home, cool he went to school. Was he sort of like a dog? If so, his choice would be German shepherd, noble and strong, with a dark muzzle.

"You feeling good?" Jordan asked tenderly.

The puppy had survived days and nights crawling along the ditch bank, drinking from puddles of murky water. Now he had a home. Now he was safe.

"You're super strong," Jordan told the dog, rising to his feet. He looked around the house for the other puppy. He found her asleep in a large cardboard box on the floor near the pantry, her tiny body nestled into an old T-shirt, her head lowered on her paws. He wished he had his phone to take a picture to send to Antonio—no, to Sierra. A sleeping puppy would melt a girl's heart.

"No phone, no life," Jordan mumbled. His mother had ordered a new one, but it wouldn't arrive for two days. Now he felt unconnected to the outside world. Was that a good thing?

Jordan examined his left hand: the knuckles were red and the back was throbbing. In the kitchen, he ran cold water over it, then dried it off on a clean dish towel. Still, the pain continued.

He looked out of the kitchen window when he heard his mom's car pull into the driveway. He went outside, expecting that she might need help with the groceries. Sure enough, she had bought a large flat of puppy milk, along with some other bulk purchases, from Costco.

"How was school?" his mom asked.

"Eerie," he replied, reaching into the trunk. He took the puppy milk under one arm and a large bag of pinto beans under the other, then started up the front porch steps.

"What do you mean?" his mom asked.

"I don't know. It's like no one really talked to me."

"And people usually talk to you?"

"Yeah, like that's all we do, Mom—talk and eat potato chips and donuts."

"Nutritious."

Mrs. Mendoza entered the house first, nudging the front door open with her shoe. When she saw one of the puppies tottering toward her, her face lit up.

"There you are, you little precious booger!" She placed her bags of groceries on the couch and bent down to pick up the pup. "Adorable!"

Jordan closed the front door after them. He took the milk and beans to the kitchen, set them on a chair, then returned to the living room. "Was I adorable when I was little?"

His mother pinched his cheek and ruffled his hair.

"Of course you were adorable."

"What am I now?"

"Handsome."

So you go from adorable to handsome?

Mrs. Mendoza carried the wandering pup back to the cardboard box by the pantry. She put him down gently, then petted his sleeping sister. "He's getting better," she remarked. "I can tell. He'll fill out."

"So," Jordan asked, curious now, "you go from adorable to handsome and then what?"

"Then you get a job and go to work, Jordan," she answered, laughing.

That night Jordan did his homework at the kitchen table, then checked his email on the family computer. Of the thirteen new emails, only one meant something: an update from Coach. The team they had played—the Tigers—had been disqualified because one of the players was an eighth grader.

"An eighth grader," Jordan whispered to himself. "That's cheating."

Jordan pushed his chair away from the computer, then drained his lukewarm hot chocolate in a single, throat-bobbing gulp.

He borrowed his mother's phone to call Antonio.

"What's up, bro?" Antonio asked. In the background Jordan could hear the music of Crazy Fruit, an indie group that Antonio had discovered last year. He'd claimed then that they were going to become bigger than Justin Bieber and Taylor Swift combined. But as far as Jordan knew, nobody else but Antonio liked them.

Jordan explained the disqualification.

"Sweet. Means you guys are the champs. Like, your mess-up didn't really count!"

"Mess-up?" Jordan fumed. "Tony, are we friends?"

"We drink from the same soda can, don't we?"

"Are you, like, *my* friend?" Jordan didn't appreciate how Antonio could be so loose in his description of what went down last Thursday.

"Bro, you're right," Antonio agreed. "But look at it this way. 'Mess-up' is better than eff-up."

Jordan hung up without a goodbye. Nanoseconds later, another email from Coach popped up on the computer screen. All players were required to show up for practice tomorrow—Tuesday—right after school. Their season would continue.

Jordan felt relieved. He did sort of mess up. But maybe he could redeem himself. Maybe he could change the outcome of the playoffs.

As he stood up, he accidentally hit his knuckles against the computer desk. "Ow!" he barked. He winced, counted to ten, then examined his hand. It was swollen, throbbing as if some hip-hop music were playing under his skin. And it was hot—really hot.

He showed his hand first to his mother, then his father.

"You gotta see the doctor," Mr. Mendoza advised. "Tomorrow. Mom will take you."

Mrs. Mendoza felt Jordan's face, from cheek to brow to nose. "Dad's right. You're going to the doctor."

At that moment, the two puppies tipped over their

cardboard box. They tumbled out, righted themselves, then began to totter toward the Mendozas. Jordan's mom scooped them both up and pressed them against her heart. Jordan whined like a dog to tease her.

7

DR. CRUZ pulled on a pair of examination gloves. He took Jordan's swollen hand between his own gloved hands, turned it palm upright, then turned it over again. He asked Jordan to shed his hoodie, which Jordan did slowly—his hand was really killing him now. The doctor looked up and down Jordan's arm. He pursed his mouth, then trailed his finger along a reddish line that extended from Jordan's wrist to his armpit. When Dr. Cruz's finger reached the armpit, Jordan let out a squeal. He was a ticklish boy.

"Blood poisoning," the doctor remarked matter-of-factly.

Blood poisoning!

Now Jordan understood the pain he'd felt last night, a throbbing pain that kept him awake. He wished that the doctor could drain his blood, then pump some good blood back into his system—like an oil change.

"Really?" his mother asked.

"Really," said Dr. Cruz, pulling off his latex gloves. He tossed them toward a trash can and both went in—swish. "How did you get those scrapes on your hand? A fight?"

Jordan hesitated, then answered, "A basketball game."

He told the doctor how he had punched a wall in anger.

"Sorry about your team's loss, but you don't get blood poisoning from punching a wall."

"It could have been the canal, I guess," said Jordan, slipping back into his hoodie.

The doctor looked confused.

"You see," Jordan explained, "I had to save this puppy." He described the incident at the canal.

"To save a puppy," Dr. Cruz said. "That's a new one."

"It's true," Jordan's mother cut in.

"That's probably the cause, then," Dr. Cruz replied. "Lots of bacteria in that sort of water." He began typing at his computer, only half listening as Mrs. Mendoza outlined the rescue of the second puppy.

"You'll have to get a penicillin shot," Dr. Cruz said, standing up. "Third floor, the lab. Plus visit the pharmacy for some pills. It's all in the computer." He handed Mrs. Mendoza some paperwork.

"You don't have, like, some stuff to put on my hand?" Jordan asked. He hated shots.

"Sorry, young man, but this requires an injection. I want you to take it easy."

"Take it easy! I can't. I'm playing ball!"

"Ball?"

"Basketball, like I told you. For the school team."

"Are you a starter?" inquired Dr. Cruz.

That really hurt; hurt more than his injured hand.

"I don't know. Maybe."

"But he can play, right?" Mrs. Mendoza asked, draping her arm around Jordan's shoulders.

"As soon as the swelling goes down."

Dr. Cruz left the room. Through the open door, Jordan could hear a boy down the hall, crying his heart out.

Jordan arrived at school two hours late, his arm in a sling. Wherever he turned, he saw Sierra. One moment she was uncapping her water bottle in the hallway. The next, she was looking at a bulletin board near the entrance to Main Hall. Jordan spied her exiting English class—she was unwrapping an energy bar, which meant that she was getting ready for algebra.

Just after second break, Sierra peered into Jordan's eyes for two full seconds. She blinked twice during this encounter. They were near the library—she was exiting while he was heading in. Jordan hesitated, wondering whether those two quick blinks meant anything deep.

Then the *moment* arrived.

"Hi," Sierra said as she passed him. Then she turned her head and added, "Sorry about your hand."

She knows about my hand? Jordan asked himself, too stunned to offer a reply. He leapt up the stairs of the library, forgot why he had come there, then exited in confusion.

How could Sierra have known that he'd hurt his hand? With his arm was in a sling, she could have said something about his arm. But no, she'd said *hand*.

Why was he even in her thoughts? Who could have told her? At this, an unpleasant image appeared in his head: blabbermouth Antonio, of course. But if it got Sierra to notice him, then Jordan was glad that his friend had crowed about the injury. Now if only Antonio would divulge his new talent at saving puppies. How could someone as sweet as Sierra not be sympathetic then?

At basketball practice, the gym echoed with the thick sounds of bouncing balls, of boys pounding from one end of the court to the other. From the ceiling, the heating ducts blasted warm air. Coach Ramirez believed that athletes should sweat to get into condition.

Jordan approached his coach, who looked up from his clipboard.

"What's this?" he asked, scowling at Jordan's sling.

"An infection."

Coach narrowed his eyes at Jordan, as if to say *This is no time for infections.* Then he asked for an explanation.

"You see," said Jordan, "I saw this puppy in the canal and he was like—"

"Mendoza," Coach said roughly. "I don't have time for a tall tale. We got a game to play—an important game."

He pointed to the banners that hung high on the gym's wall. "I want to add to them, don't you?"

"Me too, Coach."

"Then what's with the sling, and this story about a puppy?"

"It's true. I saved this puppy. You know the McKinley Street canal?"

"Oh yeah," Coach said sarcastically, beating the clipboard against his thigh. "Is that the place where teenage boys go to picnic and then—for the fun of it—drown?" Coach shook his head. "Saved a puppy, right."

"Honest, Coach," said Jordan, crossing his heart. "You remember when I punched the wall?"

"No," Coach replied, momentarily distracted by the boys on the court, "but I remember when you missed the layup."

Jordan's face fell.

Coach grimaced. "Sorry," he offered. "I really didn't mean to say that."

Jordan was silent.

"Look, Mendoza," Coach continued, "people miss baskets all the time."

Jordan brooded. *But people make baskets all the time too. Am I that weak a player?*

Coach patted Jordan's shoulder. "We got a game in a couple days. You'll play great."

Play great? He wondered. How could he, if he was still injured? And would he get any real minutes? Not come off the bench?

Coach pointed at Jordan's sling. "When does it come off?"

"Right now, if you want."

"Nah, leave it on. Your girlfriend probably likes you wearing it."

Jordan's jaw fell slowly open. *What did Coach just say?* He let some lovely thoughts rumble inside him. Then he asked, "Since when do I have a girlfriend?"

Coach glared at Jordan. "I was playing with you. You don't have a girlfriend. But you do have a nice shot within the paint." He brought a whistle to his mouth and blew hard.

Then he turned and clapped his hands loudly. The boys picked up the basketballs and gathered at center court. Coach glanced back as he walked toward the huddling players. "Stick around, Mendoza," he said. "We might need you."

8

AFTER WATCHING PRACTICE, Jordan walked home lost in a daydream. He and Sierra were on a beach, playing tag with the sudsy waves that washed in and out. They ran playfully from the waves that rolled over their bare feet. Above, seagulls honked. On the distant water, a long ship half lost in fog blared its horn. The sun cast a silvery light. Then a bottle washed ashore. He retrieved it and discovered a scroll-like message inside. He read the message: *Love is forever as long as it lasts.*

Jordan was still daydreaming three blocks from home when he heard a familiar voice call, "Hey, fool!"

"'Hey fool' yourself," said Jordan as he and Antonio bumped fists. "What's up?"

"Nada. Fact, I'm so bored I think I'm gonna do my homework."

"That bored?"

"Honestly, I wish I could be like you."

"What do you mean?"

Antonio unwrapped a lollipop and stuck it like a

spoon into the corner of his mouth. "I mean, come on, Sierra likes you."

"She does?" Jordan croaked.

"I heard her talking about you with her friend Ashley."

"They were talking about *me*?"

"Nah, just messing with you."

Jordan stomped one foot. "Man, how come you're like that?" He was angry, yet not really angry. Antonio was a joker. What else could he expect?

"'Cause we're friends." Antonio held out a fist for Jordan to bump again.

Jordan kept his hands at his sides until Antonio reached into one pocket, brought out a lollipop, and wagged it in the air. Jordan accepted the gift and stowed it in his hoodie. This wasn't the time, he thought, to coat his teeth with sugar.

Antonio took his own lollipop out of his mouth and looked seriously at Jordan. "I already told you," he began, "Sierra is, like, in love with *me*."

"Tony, get outta here!" Jordan yelled.

"I'm serious!" Antonio yelled back, even louder. "In fact, she's got posters of me and this other dude on her wall." He put the lollipop back in his mouth.

"In your dreams!" Jordan scoffed. "Go do your homework." But he was curious—*two* posters on the wall? "Who's the other dude?" he asked.

"SpongeBob!" Antonio laughed. The lollipop shot from his mouth and shattered on the curb. *"Ay, papi."*

Back home on the couch, Jordan held the puppies in the crook of his one good arm. "You're lucky you're dogs," he whispered. "You don't have to go to school, mess up in basketball, figure out what to wear every day, or fall in love—stuff like that."

He stopped cuddling the puppies and unwrapped the lollipop. He stuck it into his mouth—strawberry flavored. He placed the puppies on the floor and watched them wander away, poking their noses around the furniture. *Dogs are like people*, he thought, *using all of their senses*. But seeing the pups' noses at work, he realized that the sense of smell was most important to them.

Another question occurred to him. Was *love* a sense? In one of his rare moments of attention in Mr. Hoogasian's biology class, he had learned that sight, touch, hearing, taste, and smell were senses. But had his teacher been holding back some valuable knowledge?

Jordan heard his mother's car pull into the driveway. She tapped the horn, a signal that she had groceries. He skipped down the porch steps to help.

"How was your day?" she asked, handing Jordan two large paper bags.

"I fell in love," Jordan confessed.

"That's nice," his mother replied, not taking him seriously. "Was it with history or algebra?"

Jordan ignored this. Like Antonio, his mom could be a joker.

"And," he continued, "I realized that love might be a sixth sense."

Mrs. Mendoza raised her eyebrows. "The things we learn at school."

Jordan decided not to force the conversation. For now, he would keep quiet about Sierra. Hugging the groceries to his chest with his good arm, he sprinted up the porch steps. Then, using one foot, he held the screen door open for his mother.

"After you, my lady," he said gallantly.

"Such a gentleman," his mother declared, adopting an English accent.

Jordan was secretly pleased with himself. He had rescued two puppies and was in love. What could be better? He looked inside the grocery bags. A big carton of his favorite ice cream—butter pecan.

After the groceries were put away, Mrs. Mendoza led Jordan to the living room.

"Sit," she ordered.

He dropped onto the couch.

"I bought a lottery ticket," she announced. "I feel

lucky." She put a finger to her mouth and whispered, "But shhhhh. Don't tell Dad."

"But what if we win ten million dollars?"

Mom bit her lower lip, a sign that she was thinking. "OK, then we'll tell him."

"But what if it's, like, only five million?"

"That's easy," she laughed. "We won't say a word!"

His mother scratched the lottery ticket. Her eyes got big. "We won!" she shouted.

Jordan jumped up from the couch. "We did? How much?"

"Guess," she said, placing the winning ticket against her chest.

"Mom—come on! Tell me."

"OK, OK." She looked from Jordan to the lottery ticket, then to one of the puppies meandering near the television, and finally back to Jordan. "Twenty-five dollars."

Jordan narrowed his eyes. "Are you telling the truth??"

She shrugged and showed hm the ticket. "What can I say?"

Jordan had imagined an amount that would take them on a world cruise. But twenty-five dollars? That wouldn't even gas up the family car.

"And you know where it's going?"

He shrugged. "To buy more lottery tickets?"

"That's one idea," said his mother. "But no." She

thumbed the lottery ticket. "It's going into your college savings fund."

"My what?"

"We have a bank account for when you go to college."

Jordan was touched. His parents were thinking ahead. They could imagine a time when he had outgrown his present age—thirteen years old and counting.

"How much do I have in my fund right now?"

"Forty-four dollars."

Forty-four dollars! "But, Mom . . ."

"I know, I know," said his mother. "You're my son. There's no reason to thank me."

Mrs. Mendoza walked into the kitchen, where she stuck the lottery ticket onto the refrigerator with a magnet. Then she started dinner, opening a can of tuna while singing a really old song, a song that was a hit in the 90s.

9

BAD NEWS: the phone he'd wanted was out of stock. Jordan would have to live without it for three more days.

Whatever, he thought. These days his dreams were way better than a phone. He closed his eyes and revisited that moment when Sierra had descended the steps of the library, her most precious hand on the handrail—that lucky handrail. She'd said *hi* and followed up with *sorry about your hand*. Wasn't that sweet? And she'd blinked several times at him—there had to be meaning there!

When he opened his eyes, he was back at the kitchen table, doing his Spanish homework. He wrote, *Yo adoro.* He murmured, *"Te amo."* He whispered, *"Tengo hambre."* Then he scratched his chin. "Nah," he said. "That's gotta be wrong."

But he did adore and love Sierra, so maybe he was hungry too. He was thinking about raiding the pantry when his mother called from the other room, "Jordan—we need you!"

Jordan scooted back in his chair, stood up, and shot an imaginary three-point basket. Then he made his way to the living room.

"What's up?"

His parents were seated together cozily on the couch, like boyfriend and girlfriend. Between them squirmed the puppies.

"Seriously," his mother announced, "it's time to name them."

The puppies wagged their tails at Jordan's sudden appearance.

"You have suggestions?" his father asked.

"Remember," his mom cautioned, "names are forever, *mi'jo.*"

Jordan sat on the floor, cross-legged. "Maybe Hercules for the dude pup?"

"I don't know," his dad said. "There's only one Hercules in this house." He pointed at Jordan, face shining with pride. "You did good, son. Jumping in and saving this one." He held the male pup in his lap. "But Hercules? Nah."

"How 'bout Taylor for the girl pup?"

"You mean, like the singer?" his mom asked.

"Yeah," Jordan said. "Like the singer."

Mrs. Mendoza considered the puppy, who was nibbling at a button on her sweater. She wagged her head and said, "Too common."

They took turns making suggestions: Fluffy, Brownie, Hip-Hop (the boy pup had a swagger), Sammy, Rover,

Polo, Latte, Penny, Fido, Scout, and dozens of other dog-friendly names. Jordan's dad even tried Menudo. But none of the names seemed to fit the puppies.

Finally they arrived at Benny for the boy and Frances for the girl, in honor of pets from his parents' childhoods.

"Benny?" asked Jordan. "You had a dog named Benny?"

"Actually," his mom replied, "a cat."

"You're naming our pup after a cat?"

"He was a beautiful orange cat."

Jordan looked at his father. "And you had a dog named Frances?"

"Actually, it was a parrot."

"A *parrot*?"

"A two-toned parrot—green and yellow." Jordan's father cast his eyes toward the ceiling. "She just flew away one day." He grabbed Frances's snout and shook it like a hand. "But you, little booger, you're not flying anywhere."

My parents are a mystery, Jordan thought. He had so many questions. "How," he asked, "did you come up with my name?"

"I don't remember," his mother said.

"You don't remember?"

Mrs. Mendoza looked at her husband. "Do you remember?"

"Nah." He shook his head. "I don't remember either."

Jordan's mother clapped her hands suddenly, the bracelets jangling on her wrists. "Now I do," she said. "We were going to call you Harold."

"Harold! That's like an old man's name."

"Careful there," his dad warned. "I have an Uncle Harold."

"You do?"

"Well, I did." His eyes floated toward the ceiling again. "He's no longer with us." Mr. Mendoza crossed himself, then kissed a knuckle.

"Then we thought of naming you Lester," Mrs. Mendoza said.

"Lester! Really?" Jordan guessed that there hadn't been anyone named Lester since dinosaurs roamed the earth.

"No, wait a minute, *vieja*," said Mr. Mendoza, patting his wife on the wrist. "We were going to name him Harold . . . Lester . . . Mendoza."

"Nah, Dad, you're jokin'. I know you are." Jordan was smiling like a pumpkin.

Mrs. Mendoza bounced Frances on her lap. "That's right," she said. "Harold Lester. Or was it Lester Harold? Can't remember." She tried to hide her smile, then looked up, wiping a tear of laughter from her left eye.

"Those are nice, honorable names," his father claimed as he too dabbed at the corner of one eye. "But in the end we named you Jordan."

"After someone you knew?"

"No," said his father. "When you were born, you just looked like a Jordan."

My parents are too weird, Jordan concluded. He returned to the table, gathered up his homework, then disappeared into his bedroom, admiring the sports posters on the walls. He wanted to call Antonio, and reached into his back pocket for his phone before remembering it was dead.

Jordan heard his mom's phone ring.

"Jordan!" she called. "It's Tony."

"Coming," he shouted, not in the least surprised.

In the dining room, Jordan nearly tripped on one of the puppies. He picked it up and saw that it was Benny. The pup was small in his hand: a warm, beautiful, living thing.

He went into the kitchen and handed Benny to his mother. Then he took the phone from her.

"What's up?"

"Enchiladas tonight," Antonio informed his friend. "Red ones. How 'bout you?"

"Noodles with tuna."

"Noodles with tuna? Like, what's that taste like?"

"Pretty good. And I ate this huge bowl of ice cream."

"What flavor?"

"Butter pecan."

"Me, I had butterscotch pudding."

"That sounds good," Jordan said.

Then Antonio's voice grew serious. He revealed that Ryan Greene, the team's center, had made some rude remarks about Jordan on TikTok.

"What did he say?"

Antonio hesitated, then answered, "That you're weak."

Jordan's heart sank. That was about the worst thing a teammate could say. Did the others feel the same way? He changed the subject. "Those puppies I saved—we came up with names for them."

"And?"

"Benny for the boy and Frances for the girl."

"Human names—that's good."

Jordan then revealed that his parents had almost named him Harold Lester or Lester Harold. They couldn't remember which.

"For reals?"

"Yeah, for reals," Jordan said, fighting off a disturbing image of an angry Ryan Greene before adding, "Maybe I am weak."

"Nah, man, don't go there. You're one of the best players. You just missed, like once." Antonio apologized for bringing up the video on TikTok. Then he apologized for teasing Jordan about his feelings for Sierra. "When I told my mom what I told you, she got super mad. She said that we shouldn't play with other people's emotions." He paused for a moment, then asked, "You ain't, like, angry, are you?"

"Nah, not really," Jordan said. He was OK with Antonio, but not with Ryan.

"What's happening with your new phone?"

"A couple more days," Jordan replied.

They talked for a few more minutes, until Jordan's mom, wiggling her fingers at him, signaled that she required her phone right that second. He ended the call, then picked up the pups and carried them toward the cardboard box. It was bedtime.

In bed, Jordan assembled an image of Sierra in his mind. He hugged a pillow to his chest, then two pillows, then went back to a single pillow.

Everything was fine until he realized that he had forgotten to brush his teeth. He rolled his tongue slowly over his front and back molars, then told himself, "That's good enough."

But the moment was ruined. Behind his closed eyelids, he saw Ryan Greene again. Ryan was heading toward the backboard, holding the ball in both hands. He was readying himself for a massive dunk.

"Forget him," Jordan growled sleepily. He pulled the covers up to his chin, kissed the pillow, then fell asleep.

10

IN THE DREAM, Jordan and Sierra were sitting on a 49ers football blanket on the bank of the canal. He had brought two sodas for them and a single peanut butter and jelly sandwich cut in perfect halves.

"Do you think of me?" Jordan asked.

"All the time," Sierra answered, gazing at him.

The surface of the canal was golden with light. Occasionally, a fleet of fallen leaves floated by like unsinkable boats. Two birds quarreled in a faraway tree. A dog howled in a nearby yard. A rooster crowed, then immediately went quiet.

"You mean, like, every day?"

"Every hour of the day," Sierra corrected him.

"Every minute of the day?"

"Every second," Sierra answered.

Jordan's dream-self considered asking *How about every nanosecond?* but he managed to stop his tongue. He didn't want to hear her snap, *Jordan, give it a rest!* But, his dream-self continued, my darling would never snap like that.

Sierra briefly took his hand into hers. Then she smiled, rose to her feet, and walked away, scanning the canal. "So this is where you rescued the puppies?"

"I rescued one puppy and found the other," Jordan said, rising and following her. If he'd had a tail in the dream, it would've been wagging. Was that why they called it *puppy love*?

Sierra turned to him. "You're a hero, huh?"

Jordan became bashful. "Well, maybe."

"No maybes about it! A hero!"

Jordan lowered his eyes. "OK," he agreed. "I am."

"You know what a hero gets?"

Jordan's knees buckled. *A longish hug?*

Sierra approached until her face was a few inches from his. "Close your eyes," she said.

Jordan closed his eyes. *A . . . kiss?*

"And keep them closed."

Through the darkness of his closed eyes, Jordan smelled something good. *Do all girls wear yummy perfume?* he wondered.

"Open your mouth," Sierra ordered.

Jordan parted his lips slightly.

"More."

He opened wider.

"No, lots more! Come on, Hero Boy."

Because he had never kissed a girl before, Jordan thought that maybe you were supposed to start big, then close your mouth before receiving a peck, and then a second peck and a third peck? *Yeah*, he thought. *That must be it.*

"How's this?" he asked behind closed eyes. His mouth was wide open, like he was shouting.

"Perfect," cooed Sierra.

Jordan felt something on his tongue, something sweet and dry and smooth and crumbly all at the same time. He closed his mouth and recognized what it was right away.

"Do you like it?" Sierra asked.

Jordan chewed and swallowed. When he opened his eyes, there was Sierra in all her glory, holding one half of the peanut butter and jelly sandwich.

"It tastes good," Jordan said, licking his lips.

Sierra kissed Jordan on each check, then playfully wiped the crumbs from his face.

So this is what love tastes like, Jordan thought. *Peanut butter and jelly.*

11

WEDNESDAY MORNING, Jordan ate two bowls of sugary cereal—"rocket fuel," he called it—and brushed his teeth hard to make up for what he failed to do the previous night.

"Let me see your hand," his mother said. "Hmm." She nodded. "Looks better." Then she wrapped it several times with fresh gauze. "Dr. Cruz said you don't have to wear the sling anymore, but you're still my baby." His mom drove him to school, slowly, with both hands on the wheel.

"I had a weird dream," he told her in the car.

"A weird dream? Tell me more."

"It was about a girl."

Mrs. Mendoza raised her eyebrows. "And you like this girl?"

Jordan ignored her question. "She was feeding me a peanut butter and jelly sandwich."

"That's so sweet! What flavor jelly?"

Jordan grumbled inside. *It's useless talking to Mom.* He peered out the car window: middle-school students strolled down the sidewalk singularly and in herds. He wondered if any of them ever felt like him, confused in love and so-so at basketball.

As they approached the school, his mom tried to restart their conversation. "See?" she said, keeping both eyes on the road. "It's not so bad living without a phone."

"Yeah," Jordan agreed, falsely. He was dying without a phone. Then he spotted Sierra with Antonio. They were walking side by side like—he could hardly believe it—like boyfriend and girlfriend. Jordan felt a stab of jealousy right in the heart.

"What's wrong?" his mom asked as she turned on her blinkers and slowed the car, just short of the school entrance. She didn't like getting tangled in the morning traffic, the long centipede of cars creeping slowly up the school driveway to deliver their students, then inching slowly back down to the main road.

"Nothing," Jordan answered.

Mrs. Mendoza navigated to the curb and parked. She turned to Jordan, played with his hair, and promised, "Don't worry, your phone will arrive soon—maybe even today." She kissed her son on the forehead and felt his nose. "Good," she said. "It's cool. You're not sick."

Jordan hustled toward school, his backpack bouncing on his shoulders. Each smack reminded him of the slaps on the back he would get when he was little and choking on something—a peanut butter and jelly sandwich came to mind. The inability to breathe always scared him. But his mother would pound his back until his throat cleared and he could inhale again. By then, his eyes were watery. At the moment, his eyes also were watery—but not from lack of breath. His best friend had his arm wrapped around Sierra's shoulders!

"I saw you," Jordan told Antonio.

"It ain't what you think."

"Like you hugging her ain't nothin'?"

"Hugging her? You crazy."

"Like, dude—I saw."

The two boys were standing near a drinking fountain draped with a plastic bag. It had been broken since the start of school, three months earlier. These days everyone survived on their own water bottle, so who cared about a broken drinking fountain?

"I gotta explain. She was super sad."

Jordan stared at his friend.

"Bro, like her dog died. I just wanted to make her feel better and—"

"Her dog died?" Jordan interrupted.

"Last night."

Jordan's anger drained out of him. He suddenly felt like a jealous fool.

"She and her mom buried the dog this morning."

Groaning, Jordan pictured Sierra rolling the dog into a grave. He knew very well the feeling when you had to bury a dog.

"Ah, bro, I messed up—I'm really sorry." He had misread a natural response, what any caring person would have done—when someone feels sad, you try to offer comfort, a shoulder to cry on. He apologized again and told Antonio that he was the best dude ever.

"That's cool."

After a moment of silence, Jordan asked, "How did the dog die?"

"It was like hecka old." Antonio reached into a pocket for his phone, looked at a message, then returned the phone to his pocket. He asked, "How are the puppies?"

The first bell rang. At the same time, an idea sounded in Jordan's head, reverberating from one brain cell to the next. *Puppies!* His face glowed, his heart leapt. Again, he apologized to Antonio.

"Like I said, it's cool."

The two boys bumped fists and started toward their first-period classes.

In language arts, Jordan disappeared behind his notebook like a gopher diving into his hole. He needed privacy, a place inside himself where he could figure out how to offer Sierra a puppy as a gift. But first he would have to get to know her. He couldn't just go up to her and say, "Hey, it's me, Mr. Basketball. You know, the guy who missed that clutch shot!"

When Mrs. Roosevelt asked Jordan to read a passage from their assigned novel, he did it almost perfectly, though he couldn't have told anyone what the words he'd read aloud might mean. *Who cares about books*, he thought, *when you're in love?* There was no one in the world who could possibly feel what he was feeling.

During break, Jordan began to explain his plans to Antonio, then stopped himself. They were on the abandoned basketball courts on the south side of campus. The nets were gone and the rims bent. Weeds pushed up from the cracks in the asphalt. Still, this was where the two of them always hung during morning break. For the afternoon break, they moved to the steps of the library. They only entered the library when there was homework to do.

"I know you wanna say something," Antonio said, his breath visible in the cold. "Like, what is it?"

"I can't say."

"WHAT! I'm your *carnal*. You can tell me anything." Antonio appeared to reconsider these words. "Unless you're asking me for some coin. Because, like, I don't got none." He told Jordan that he was saving money to buy a new game called *Your Face in Space*.

Jordan was suddenly uninterested in video games. His new focus in life was Sierra Mendez. In the end, he described his idea to Antonio. He would give Sierra one of the puppies. Then they would have something in common—puppies that would grow into noble dogs.

"*Suave*," Antonio said, stroking his chin thoughtfully. "Genius. No wonder you're getting that row of Cs on your report card."

"Yeah, genius." Jordan was feeling good. He had the sudden urge to pound his chest like King Kong.

"Genius," Antonio went on, "except for this one thing."

"What?"

"She's not thinking 'bout getting another dog. She's feeling sad that she just put hers in the ground. Know what I mean?"

The King Kong moment passed. "Yeah," Jordan said. "You're right."

"Plus, dude, ain't the pups just a couple weeks old?"

"Yeah, real little, like just starting off."

"Still, they need to grow before you give 'em away." He reached into the pocket of his hoodie and brought out a candy bar. He bared his front teeth like a gopher and tore the package open. "Plus, there's something else."

"What is that?" Jordan asked.

"Your mom." Antonio bit into the candy bar, then chewed for the longest time. "You told me she loves them puppies. She wouldn't give one up."

True. The puppies were like newborn babies to his

mother. She even fed them from small baby bottles. There was some serious bonding going on there.

Jordan would have discussed the situation more if Ryan Greene and two of his friends hadn't appeared. They walked slowly over to Jordan and Antonio.

"Looks like your hand's still messed up," Ryan said.

Jordan held up his hurt paw, still wrapped in gauze. "Yeah."

"That's good," Ryan smirked, then spat.

"Why is it good?" Jordan asked.

"Because now"—Ryan snickered—"we have a chance to win."

"How come you gotta say that?"

"You know why."

"I do?" Jordan said, closing his good hand into a fist.

"Like"—Ryan snickered again—"you won't be able to miss another basket." He took a step toward Jordan, looking taller than ever. "But it don't matter that you missed. We're still in the playoffs."

"People miss baskets all the time," Antonio said.

"Really? All the time?" Ryan said with a sneer. "That's only if you're Jordan Mendoza. Always throwing up bricks."

Jordan charged as the break bell sounded, as if it were ringing an end to round one. But the fight was just beginning.

12

WHEN RYAN had taunted him, Jordan wasn't about to back down. Now *both* of his hands were injured and his jaw, left ear, and all of his ribs hurt. He had taken some roundhouse blows, including one to the face, but he had given back too. He remembered what his dad had told him, how someone can be tall but not big. That was Ryan, a straight-up six-footer. And that's why Jordan had pounded Ryan with shots to the gut, the nearest available target. He had doubled over momentarily, the breath knocked out of him, but then he had landed a solid punch to the side of Jordan's head. That last one, Jordan admitted to himself, had really hurt. Tears had sprung into his eyes, then he tottered backward and fell. That ended the fight.

Now, with the school day over, Jordan stood on the sidelines of the gym, wearing street clothes. He was still a member of the team and was expected to show up for practice. He felt nervous. Would Ryan start another brawl? Jordan had held his own, but Ryan's jabs and windmill punches could deliver real pain.

The players were warming up, shouting loudly to each other. Some leapt into the air as they brought their knees up to their chests. Some ran from one end of the court to the other. They were getting ready for whatever drills Coach had devised for them, ready to win.

Ryan appeared, seeming to be in a subdued mood. He immediately swiveled his head toward Jordan. His eyes didn't hold the rage they had earlier; instead, they were dark buttons. His mouth was closed, his lips a gray line.

Coach Ramirez appeared from the locker room, hugging four basketballs. He let them roll from his arms onto the floor, where they were scooped up by the boys. The team began to pass the balls around and dribble, the sound of the balls like thunder against the floor.

"Jordan, get your butt over here," Coach snapped. "You too, Ryan."

The two slowly approached. Neither wanted to arrive first to the scolding. They sidled up to Coach, who looked from one to the other before placing a hand on each of their shoulders.

"I heard you two were fighting," Coach said. "What was that about?"

The boys shrugged.

Coach shrugged back, mocking them. "So that's your answer?" He shrugged again. "Fighting is stupid. You're teammates."

"But," Jordan began, "he said—"

Coach cut him off. "I don't care what Ryan said—or

what you said. No fighting. We have a game tomorrow." Coach grimaced at Jordan's bandaged hand. "It still hurts?"

"Yeah." Jordan raised his hand. He slowly clenched and unclenched his fingers, a movement that indeed hurt. "But it's feelin' better."

"Feelin' better?" Coach smirked. "Yeah, right." Then he told the boys to shake hands.

"I was wrong," Ryan said, squeezing Jordan's hand in his, not in a mean way but with sincerity. "I took the post down."

"Thanks, man," said Jordan. Then, touching his left ear, he added, "Like, my ear was ringing all through civics."

Ryan placed one palm over his stomach. "Yeah, you got me good."

They bumped fists and were teammates again, though Jordan was forced to sit on the sidelines, alone, without a phone to scroll. From the bleachers, he watched the practice and recognized, as if for the first time, that his team was really strong. Ryan, Jordan had to admit, was the heart of the team—the one who called plays, who scrambled for loose balls. He was tall and he also wasn't afraid of getting knocked around. They had a good chance, Jordan thought, of beating the Falcons.

"Hey," a voice called. It was Antonio, walking toward him with his shoelaces dragging. In one hand, a foot-long churro. In the other hand, his phone. He climbed into the bleachers.

"You want some?" Antonio asked, holding up the churro like a candle.

"Hey, Tony. Nah, I'm good," Jordan answered. He wasn't hungry. Prior to Antonio's arrival, he had been repeatedly opening and closing his injured hand, exercising it. *Who knows*, he thought. *Maybe Coach will put me in the game tomorrow.*

Normally, Jordan wasn't a starter, but Pedro Avila, their usual starting guard, wasn't at practice. Why, he wasn't sure. *Maybe Coach will have to call on me.* He was nervous about this. He would absolutely have to come through next time. He continued to watch his teammates on the court while Antonio scrolled his phone and devoured his crunchy churro.

13

"**HEY, DAD,**" Jordan greeted his father, who was lounging in his recliner. The TV was off, but Mr. Mendoza, eyes closed after a long day, had the remote in his hand. He opened his eyes, smiled, stretched, then yawned. Jordan plopped down on the ottoman beside him. It was time to talk.

Jordan's father yawned again. "How was school?"

"Pulling down Cs," Jordan answered.

"That good, huh?"

"Yeah," Jordan said, with a slight smile. "That good." He hesitated, then announced, "I got a problem."

"You're not still upset about missing that layup, are you?" Mr. Mendoza sat up in his recliner and rubbed his tired eyes. He woke before sunrise and after two cups of coffee was out the door to his job as a plumber. There was always a faucet dripping in somebody else's kitchen or a toilet overflowing onto the bathroom floor. Sometimes he had to crawl under houses to check for leaking pipes; other times he had to peer above false ceilings. Whenever he installed a new sink, he carted away the old one on a hand dolly. His ordinary injuries included scraped knuckles, a sore back, and painful knees. Once, when the valve on a water heater burst, the skin on his neck and chin were badly scalded.

"Yeah, I am," Jordan sighed, "but it's something else." He took a deep breath. "It's this girl."

"*No mi digas. Una muchacha?*" His father slammed a heavy hand on the arm of the recliner. "It's about time. So what's going on?"

"There's this girl . . ."

"*Pues*, you said that already. Details, *por favor*."

Jordan described Sierra by using the word *beautiful* six times and *smart* four times. He said that there was never a girl like her in the whole history of humankind.

"OK, I get it," his dad said. "You like her." He chuckled.

Jordan then confided that they were not really social, though she did say hi to him once, and had asked about his hand.

"And how is your hand?"

"Better," Jordan answered. When he got home from basketball practice, he had unraveled the bandage—torn and dirty from the fight—and discovered that the skin beneath was no longer red. He made a fist, to show his father, then opened his fingers again.

"She sounds like a pretty girl."

"Dad," Jordan complained, "you weren't listening.

Sierra is beautiful beyond words."

"OK, then 'beautiful beyond words'—nice ring to that phrase. Anyhow, unless you make a move . . ." He looked toward the kitchen, where Jordan's mom was stuffing the pots and pans she seldom used into a large plastic bag, a donation for Goodwill. "When I was your age," he continued, lowering his voice, "I was right where you are now."

Jordan stared at his father in disbelief. Of course, he told himself, his parents weren't *born* old. Not like Mr. Wilson, his algebra teacher, who could never have been an ordinary child. His nostril hairs must have hung from his nose ever since he began to eat solid food, right after the second term of Franklin D. Roosevelt.

"And I liked this girl," his dad whispered. "But she didn't know that I existed."

"What did you do?"

"I let her swim away. I was scared of saying a word." He smiled at the memory.

"Was she pretty?"

"Oh yeah!"

"Super pretty?" In Jordan's world, after pretty came super pretty, and then beautiful followed by super beautiful. After that you became a model or a movie star, got married and divorced, then signed on to a reality show.

"Beautiful," Mr. Mendoza said, raising his eyes toward the ceiling. "But you know what?"

"What?"

"I got to know her later."

"How?"

"This started when I was in junior high—eighth grade, like you—"

"I'm in seventh, Dad."

"OK, seventh." His grin widened. "But I got to know her later, in high school." He looked down at his lap, then back at Jordan. "She was your mom." He giggled and palm-slapped the arm of the recliner.

"You mean you've known Mom since eighth grade?"

"Third grade, actually. But, yeah, I liked her then and I like her now." He sighed. "She's my girl. I love her."

Jordan imagined Sierra drifting away, then coming back into his life in high school—senior year would be perfect. Then the two of them would go off to college and get married. Her maid of honor, Ashley. His best man, Antonio. He smiled inwardly as he imagined their life together. He would become a surveyor and she would become a dietitian. A job that had to do with what people ate or didn't eat. Or something like that. She ate only healthy food herself.

"So, what about this girl?" his father asked, interrupting his reverie.

Just then Mrs. Mendoza walked into the living room. She beckoned Jordan with a finger.

"I'll be back," Jordan told his dad. "Don't lose your train of thought."

He followed his mother into the kitchen.

"I want you to swipe those spiderwebs," she ordered, pointing toward the ceiling and handing him a dish towel.

Jordan climbed a chair and did as instructed, then jumped down. "Mom," he began, "I got to ask something—I mean, tell you something." He then described Sierra: a girl he liked at school, a girl who was super beautiful, a girl who hardly recognized his existence, a girl with grades that were higher than his head had been when he was standing on the chair.

When he finished talking, his mother told him to take the two large plastic bags full of kitchenware to the garage.

"You don't have anything to say to me?" Jordan was surprised. Wasn't a mother supposed to become curiously tender at discovering a son in love?

"Not really. You're just at that age."

His mom smiled when the two puppies bounded into the kitchen. She bent down and ran a hand over their sleek, warm bodies.

"You're getting bigger, huh, you little boogers. You two are so precious, even when you pee on the floor."

Jordan could see that the pups had grown bigger and stronger. They were no longer the wet, wobbly things from the canal. They had a home now, with regular feedings of puppy milk.

Mrs. Mendoza looked back up at Jordan. "So, what's her name?"

"Sierra," he answered, happy that his mom was showing some interest now.

Jordan and his mother looked at each other. She didn't ask about Sierra, and Jordan didn't volunteer any information.

"Take the garbage out too," Mrs. Mendoza said. "And don't forget to secure the lid."

The lid, Jordan knew, was to keep animals out. Cats were always on the prowl. And rats so large that their whiskers dragged on the ground. Once he had seen a rat sneaking off with a carton of Chinese takeaway.

Out in the semidarkness—the security light had come on—Jordan wondered how he could suggest giving away one of the puppies. He practiced a sentence: "Mom, Sierra's dog like died for good." He made a somber face. "And I was thinking, maybe we can give one of the puppies to her. Good idea, huh?" He imagined his mother's expression and cringed. Maybe, he thought, it would be better to make this suggestion over the phone.

As he returned to the house, Jordan heard his mom's phone ringing. He hurried up the steps, yelling, "I got it."

The phone was on the kitchen table.

He knew it would be Antonio—and he was right.

"What did you have for dinner?" his friend asked.

"Meatloaf. You?"

"Spaghetti. And spaghetti for at least two more days. My mom made enough to feed the whole school."

Their conversation lasted nearly an hour.

After the call, Jordan checked his email on his laptop. There were three daily reports from school, some junk mail about invisible braces and acne cream, and one message from Coach Ramirez. He read it twice. Coach was asking if he could play tomorrow.

"Coach wants me to play?" Jordan said softly to himself. He flexed the fingers on his left hand. The pain was still present, but it wasn't as bad as it had been earlier. He had been taking antibiotics twice daily and trying to keep his hand clean, sometimes even plunging it into a sock to wear around the house. He was definitely on the mend.

But Jordan was worried. What if he went up for another last-minute layup—or risked a shot beyond the arc—and missed? His athletic career would be completely over. He would have no choice but to join the chess club.

I'm in, Coach, he wrote back. He turned and eyed the basketball in the corner of his bedroom. He stood and picked it up, bounced it once against the carpeted floor, then squeezed it between both hands. There was a dull ache in his left hand, but no jarring pain.

Jordan retrieved his gym bag from the closet. From his chest of drawers, he pulled out a fresh-smelling jersey, a pair of socks, a sweatshirt, an athletic supporter, and two T-shirts. He packed his gear. When Benny trotted over to investigate, he playfully placed him in the bag as well. The pup sniffed Jordan's clothes, then looked up and barked.

"You're so funny, Benny," Jordan said.

The puppy yawned and laid his head on his paws.

Then Frances bounced into the bedroom. Jordan bent down and put her into the bag too. When the pups pressed their noses together, he felt an overwhelming tenderness toward them. He had saved these two siblings, but he'd had to bury the third.

When Jordan went to sleep, the pups were still in his gym bag, snoring quietly.

14

"SO YOU GONNA PLAY?" Antonio asked. They were in front of the school, leaning against a wall. The first bell had yet to ring.

Jordan flexed his hand inside its new, clean bandage of gauze. "It feels OK."

Antonio hesitated before announcing, "Pedro got hurt."

Pedro Avila, the team's best player after Ryan. So that's why Coach had sent the email. Jordan usually began the game on the bench, but he got his minutes on the court. With Pedro injured, he might get more.

"What happened?"

"A car wreck."

"Really?" Jordan had a momentary image of a car smashed into a wall, with smoke rising from under the buckled hood.

"Yeah, he had to go to the hospital. He's home now."

Jordan had known Pedro since first grade. In elementary school, he had always been the smallest kid on the playground. But then, over the summer between sixth and seventh grades, he grew a foot taller. His shoulders broadened and his biceps gleamed when he flexed them. If he pulled up his shirt, his belly showed a true six-pack.

"Like, dang!" Jordan roared when he saw Pedro at the beginning of seventh grade.

"What?" Pedro asked in a strangely deep voice.

"You're totally rock!"

Now he was hurt—and from a car crash?

Jordan's head turned when he heard a rattling chain. Two Junior ROTC cadets were raising the flag. Up the pole it went, yank by yank. And with the final yank, the flag began to wave. The school bell rang. Students hurried to class, some dropping potato chip bags into a trash can as they made their way up the steps to Main Hall.

Jordan and Antonio pushed themselves away from the wall and started off to homeroom. As he skipped up the steps, Jordan felt the contents of his gym bag shift. He took a seat in class, placing his gym bag on one side of the chair and his backpack on the other. He reached into his pack, lifted out his laptop, and turned it on. Within seconds a reflection of the monitor glowed on his face.

Mrs. Starr came into the classroom, carrying her own laptop. Her hair had a streak of blue and tattoos ringed her wrists. A lanyard with a single key hung around her neck.

"Morning, people," she said, sizing up the class. She was in a happy mood.

Other than a few half-covered yawns, the students made no response.

"What do we say?" she asked cheerfully. "Let me try again." She smiled broadly, the overhead lights glinting off her eyeglasses. "Morning, class."

This time around every pupil managed to crow "Morning"—everyone except Jordan, who had lowered his gaze to the floor. He was eyeing his gym bag, which had appeared to move, almost squirm. Had his basketball shoes taken on a life of their own? He had seen enough fantasy movies to know anything was possible. *Way creepy*, he thought.

Brent, also known as Snoopy, looked over at Jordan from the desk beside him. He mouthed the question silently: "What's up?"

Jordan responded silently, "I don't know."

Mrs. Starr, who was an excellent lip-reader, observed this exchange. "Mr. Mendoza," she inquired in a light voice, "what is it you don't know?"

"My gym bag," Jordan said.

"My gym bag," Mrs. Starr repeated in a near whisper. "What about it? No—wait. Let's find out." She made her way down the aisle to Jordan's desk. She hovered near him, then pulled up the sleeves of her sweater, revealing more tattoos. She narrowed one eye at the bag and asked, "May I?"

Jordan shrugged and said, "Yeah, I guess."

She picked up the bag, then carried it to her desk in the front of the classroom. She unzipped it. "Oh," she squeaked as a smile spread across her face. "Class, we have a guest."

When she pulled out the puppy, everyone gushed and stood up, leaning like sunflowers toward her. She held it up in one hand, as if displaying a trophy. Moments ago the students had looked sleepy, but now they were wide awake and full of life. And their phones were coming out of hiding.

"Benny!" Jordan shouted. "What are you doing here?"

"Benny," Mrs. Starr said, "that's a sweet name." Then her smile collapsed and a storm brewed behind her eyes. She pushed up the sleeves of her sweater again. "What's this dog doing here?" She slapped her own cheek playfully. "Oh, that's right, our new transfer student." The storm in her eyes became a tempest. "Is that it, Jordan Mendoza?"

Jordan swallowed fearfully. He began with the beginning. "See, I rescued this dog . . ."

"Save it," said Mrs. Starr, "for the novel you might write one day. You and Benny have an appointment to see the vice principal." She stroked the puppy, wrinkled her nose, then looked down into the gym bag. "It appears," she remarked, "that our furry guest has wet himself."

The class laughed.

"Really," Jordan mumbled as he rose from his desk, "I don't know how Benny got in there." He approached the teacher and took the puppy in his arms.

But before Jordan could leave, everyone pushed their

way to the front of the class to pet the unexpected guest. They all found him adorable—Benny the pup, that is.

Mr. Hollister was on the phone when Jordan walked into his office. He hung up and grimaced at Jordan.

"Mr. Hollister," Jordan began, "I know it looks bad, but it's not my fault."

The vice principal leaned back into his chair, which resembled the captain's seat on *Star Trek*. "You're Gregory Mendoza, correct?"

"Jordan Mendoza."

"On the basketball team, right?" He bent a paper clip into a pretzel, then tossed it into an empty coffee cup. "Now I remember. You missed the basket last Thursday."

Is that all I am? Jordan wondered. *A missed shot?* "Yeah," he said. "I'm on the team."

Mr. Hollister considered the bandage on Jordan's hand. "You broke it or something?"

"It got infected."

"Infected," Mr. Hollister repeated, then looked away as his phone rang. He answered it and listened, the corners of his mouth pulled down. "OK, right. And when? Tuesday?" He hung up. "That was a call from the Avila family."

"I know him."

"Of course you know him—star player." Mr. Hollister shook his head. "Poor kid. Broke a kneecap." He eyed

Jordan. "So why are you here?"

Jordan gazed down at his gym bag.

"It's a long story, Mr. Hollister."

"You think I have time for a long story? I don't even have time for lunch."

Jordan raised his gym bag. "There's a dog inside."

"A dog," repeated Mr. Hollister. "Now what is a dog doing inside your bag?"

"Actually, it's a puppy."

Mr. Hollister roared, "Dog, or puppy—or goldfish! You're not supposed to bring animals to school!"

The phone rang again. Mr. Hollister took it and snapped, "Yeah." He listened for a few seconds before saying, "Chocolates and flowers."

He hung up and stared blankly at Jordan for a moment, as if he couldn't remember what they had been talking about. "And why," he said finally, "would you bring a puppy to school?"

"That's part of the long story."

"Ah, Gregory."

"Jordan, Mr. Hollister," said Jordan. Then he explained, slowly and clearly, how Benny had slept in his gym bag the night before and, he guessed, liked it so much that the puppy had climbed in again this morning. Before leaving for school, he had zipped up the bag without noticing the pup.

"Mr. Mendoza, why should I believe this?"

"Because it's the truth," Jordan replied. He told how he had rescued the puppy from the canal. "And that's how," he continued, "my hand got infected."

"Jordan, Jordan, Jordan . . . I have been teaching here for sixteen years—before you were born. I've heard all sorts of stories, but this one is up there." He chuckled, a false sound. "You rescued a puppy from a canal. Brave boy."

"I swear, it's all true."

"Call your mom," Mr. Hollister ordered, turning his face to the computer screen.

Jordan hesitated. "Mr. Hollister," he began.

The vice principal looked up, the light of the computer flickering in his eyeglasses. "Now what?"

"I don't have a phone."

Mr. Hollister scowled. He took off his glasses and rubbed his eyes.

"A teenager without a phone?" He sat up straight and tossed his glasses on the desk, as if readying for a fight. "First you tell me that a dog accidentally came to school in your gym bag. Now you tell me you have no phone? That's impossible!"

"But, Mr. Hollister," Jordan said softly.

"WHAT!"

"It's not a dog—it's a puppy." Jordan glanced down at the gym bag at his feet. "You want to see him?"

"Dog! Puppy! Frog or toad! Whatever you got in your bag, I don't want to see it!" He pointed toward the door. "Tell Mrs. Wade to let you use the office phone. Now out!"

15

WHEN HIS MOTHER ARRIVED at the school office, Jordan pleaded for forgiveness. "Really, Mom," he said. "Benny just climbed in. I didn't know he was there."

Mrs. Mendoza took the puppy in her arms, cooing sweet words. But when she looked up at Jordan, her smile was gone. She was siding with Mr. Hollister.

"I'm supposed to believe that?"

"It's true, Mom." Jordan crossed his heart, then added, "Everyone likes him."

"Of course they do!" She bounced the puppy up and down, like a baby. To Jordan, she snapped, "You're lucky that I'm a nice mom."

"Totally, Mom. The best." He reached over to pet Benny, but his mother slapped his hand away.

"What time is the game?"

"Four," he answered.

"Are you playing?"

Jordan shrugged, then asked, "Are you gonna come?"

Mrs. Mendoza shrugged in return. "I don't know," she said, pretending to fume.

"You're not really mad, are you?"

"I was," she said, "but not now." Smiling again, she handed him some clean clothes and told him that she wouldn't miss his game for the world. Without putting Benny down, she wrapped one arm around Jordan's shoulders and kissed him on the cheek.

At that moment, Sierra Mendez walked into the office. She paused and looked at Jordan questioningly.

"Hi," said an embarrassed Jordan. His heart was suddenly running rabbit-fast. *This*, he realized, *was his moment.* "Sierra," he asked, "you want to see my puppy?"

"Puppy?" she replied in a quiet voice. "What do you mean a puppy?"

"He's right here." Jordan turned to his mother. "Mom, you wanna show Sierra the puppy?"

Jordan felt his heart outrun the rabbit. He had uttered her name twice in ten seconds. He was no longer just talking to his pillow—but the real living Sierra! He could read his mom's mind. She was thinking, *So this is the girl.*

Mrs. Mendoza stepped toward her, showing off Benny like a game-show prize.

"He's so cute!" Sierra cried, petting him.

"Do you mean my son, Jordan?" Mrs. Mendoza asked teasingly. She wrinkled her nose at him and stretched out a hand to play with his hair. Jordan was so mortified that he would have been happier to feel the floor swallow him whole.

A pink tinge spread across Sierra's cheeks. "How old is he?" she asked.

"You mean Jordan, star basketball player?"

"Mom!" *Please, Mom, don't say any more,* Jordan begged silently. He worried that she might start divulging the secrets of his private lifestyle next, such as his power breakfast of two bowls of Cap'n Crunch. "Mom," he said earnestly, "don't you have some . . . shopping to do?"

"Not really," she replied. "We're having leftovers for dinner." Smiling, she turned to face Sierra. "Enchiladas. Do you like enchiladas?"

"Of course."

Mrs. Mendoza looked from Sierra to Jordan and then back to Sierra. There was a twinkle in her eyes. She leaned her head toward Jordan and whispered in his ear, "Is this the girl?"

Jordan could have died—no, he would die. He closed his eyes and wished that he could start the day over. He wished that he had checked his gym bag before leaving the house. Then he opened his eyes and saw that Sierra was now glowing from embarrassment.

"The pup's name is Benny," Jordan volunteered, his mind finally starting to catch up with his heart. "He's gonna be hecka big."

Jordan took a deep breath; he was salvaging the situation. He just wished that his mom would vaporize and reassemble in another part of the world—*home* would be perfect. Maybe there was some more kitchen stuff that could be bagged and sent off to Goodwill, *pronto*.

"And how do you know Jordan?" his mother asked.

Jordan could see that Sierra was struggling.

"Ahhh," she began.

"Mom," Jordan announced, "life is calling." He led her by the elbow to the school's front door. "I gotta go to class."

"OK, OK, I'll see you at four," Mrs. Mendoza said. She waved to Sierra and called, "Nice meeting you." Then she beamed at Jordan and whispered, "She *is* the girl, huh?"

Jordan watched as his mom disappeared through the double doors, cooing to Benny. When she'd gone, he lowered his head and stared the floor. *Was there any point in living?*

Seconds passed, nearly a whole minute, before he looked up. Sierra was still standing in front of him.

She smiled at him, then asked, "Why was the puppy here, Jordan?"

Jordan inhabited a dream world for the rest of the day. Sierra had called him by his name! By next week, he might be holding her hand, hugging, and making wild promises. He was aware of only one possible complication: Sierra was a top-tier student. He would have to join in the quest to get all As. He was getting ahead of himself, however. *Maybe,* he thought, *I should try to get some Bs first.*

When the last bell sounded—another day at school done—he shouldered his backpack and swung his gym bag at his side. He left social studies, his last class. It was 2:45. Sunlight drenched the campus trees, their branches almost bare. A few leaves fell, but not many. Suddenly, in an unexpected shimmer of creative thinking, Jordan started to compose a love song.

"You mean so, so much," he sang as he walked across the bustling quad. He couldn't help being happy. On his next trip through the refrain, he stretched out the word *mean* so that it hung in the air for several seconds.

"You mean WHAT, homes?" Antonio hollered, though he was right behind Jordan.

Jordan had been trying to decide whether to replace "so much" with "a lot," "a whole lot," or "totally, wholly a lot," when his friend interrupted. His musical composition was ruined.

"Nothing," Jordan answered honestly. "I'm just singing."

"My *carnal*, singing?" Antonio circled Jordan, then said, not too quietly, "You in love! That happens all the time."

"What happens all the time?"

"People in love want to express their feelings—that's what." He suggested that Jordan learn to play three chords on the guitar. With those chords, he could sing all the

TikTok hits he wanted.

"Guitar? I don't have time to learn the guitar."

"Man, it's easy. I checked out this YouTube 'bout this chimpanzee who learned in one day."

Jordan told him to shut up.

After a few minutes of quiet, Antonio spoke up again. "I get how you feel, 'cause the one time I was in love, I was, like, singing way loud."

"Who were you in love with?" To tell the truth, Jordan couldn't imagine Antonio in love.

Antonio smiled. There was a speck of food between his two front teeth.

"Not WHO but WHAT!" He started to describe a taco truck on Tulare Street that served a torta as big as a baseball mitt.

At that moment, Jordan began to doubt the basis of their friendship. They had been tricycle dudes on the same street when they were six years old. Antonio had moved away, then moved back when his parents divorced. He and his mom now lived in a small white house a few blocks from where Jordan lived. The lawn was torn up by their dog with mismatched eyes. Roosters stirred the neighbors awake before the sun came up. His mom hung their laundry on a fence for everyone to see—on some days, Antonio's *chones* blew in the wind. *Whatever,* Jordan thought. He and Antonio went way back.

"You mean you're in love with a torta?"

"Not just any torta, but like I say, a huge, delicious torta from the state of Michoacán." Antonio spread his arms wide. "I mean, like, it can feed a family of four if you want to share. But not me—no way."

They had made their way from the quad to the front of the school. Students were hopping into their parents' cars or riding away on bikes and skateboards. But most would be waiting around for the game at 4:00. Some were sitting on benches, others were leaning against the bike racks, and two were sitting in a tree. All of them were eating potato chips and drinking sodas.

"You wanna hang?" Antonio asked, with a slight plea in his voice.

"Bro," Jordan began. "I got a game to play. I ain't got time to hang." What he didn't say was that, right now, he really needed to be alone. He hoped his best friend would understand.

"That's right," said Antonio, skipping backward. "You gotta compose that love song. See you later." He stopped, set his feet, then shot an imaginary basketball. "Swish!" he yelled. "I'm good."

After Antonio left, Jordan floated around campus for a few minutes, hoping to run into Sierra. But she was nowhere in sight. It was better that way, he thought— Coach didn't tolerate lateness. He hurried off to the gym, catching up with Ryan and two other teammates, John Poole and Manuel Lopez, both good players.

"Hey," Jordan called, jogging toward them.

The three boys turned.

"It's terrible about Pedro," Jordan remarked.

"A bummer," Ryan agreed.

Manuel asked Jordan how his hand was.

Jordan turned it over several times, testing his wrist and fingers. He told Manuel that it still hurt, then thought about the fact that he hadn't shot a basketball in nearly a week. "Honestly," he said, "I don't think I'm ready to play."

"But you would if we need you, right?" Manuel asked as they walked toward the locker room.

On the court, Andre was heading toward the basket, preparing to shoot a layup. He leapt—and missed.

"Yeah, if Coach wants me in."

"Cool," said Manuel.

They bumped fists. The Patriots were ready to tangle.

The clock was clicking down toward the end of the second quarter. The overhead lights hummed. The heater breathed out warm, dusty air. It was 24–19, the visiting Falcons in the lead. The bleachers were nearly filled with classmates and parents of both teams.

Mr. Hollister, the vice principal, appeared in the doorway. He clapped a few times, encouraging the team, and then left, head down, scowling as he talked on his phone.

Jordan sat on a squeaky folding chair watching the Patriots run up and down the court. The team's defense was bad, then good, then bad again. But they were hustling, with multiple players scrambling for loose balls.

"You can do it!" Jordan yelled. He had been nervously squeezing a towel, shouting encouragement and jumping to his feet when his team scored. Ryan had ten points, Manuel five. The other players were doing the best they could against a strong opponent.

At halftime, the team sat in a semicircle in their locker room, toweling off.

"You're doing good!" Coach Ramirez barked. "But what's the next level?"

"Better!" the team roared.

Coach talked defense—hands up, hands in front, hands spread like eagle wings at your sides. He talked pick-and-rolls and box outs. He instructed them to get the ball to Ryan whenever he was under the basket. Don't foul, he warned them, and don't try to shoot over a taller defender. Pass the ball. Keep passing the ball until a player is open.

"You OK?" Coach asked Manuel, who had taken an elbow to his face and bled some.

Manuel gently felt his nose. "Just hurts," he said. "That's all."

Andre moved closer to examine it. He took Manuel's chin in his hand and pushed his head back slightly. One eye closed, he peered up his nostrils.

Coach looked at Jordan. "How do you feel, Mendoza?"

"Good, Coach." Jordan's heart beat faster. Coach was debating whether to put him into the game.

The team returned to the court in a line, with Ryan up front. Then they huddled together, arms around each other's shoulders. They stood still for a moment, then broke their formation with a shout: "Gooooo, Patriots!"

Jordan sat down, shaded his eyes from the overhead lights, and turned to scan the bleachers. His parents were there. And Sierra and her friend Ashley were sitting a couple of rows in front of them. He swallowed. Then he saw his mom wave to Sierra and call, "Sit with us."

Jordan watched Sierra and Ashley climb over a few spectators, then sit down next to his mom and dad. "Ah, man," he muttered. What was his mother going to reveal about him? That his table manners were primitive? His bedroom a mess? His showers too long? He felt sweat running down his arms, and he hadn't even played a minute yet. There was no telling what his mother would say—or do. Share pictures of him when he was a baby? Probably the one where he was butt naked on a blanket!

Then he heard a referee's whistle and turned his head back to the court.

At the tip-off, the Patriots got the ball. In three long strides, Ryan scored with an easy layup: 24–21. Ryan turned and hustled back on defense, one fist in the air to acknowledge the foot-stomping parents and classmates in the bleachers.

A Falcons player dribbled the ball up the court and attempted to pass, but it sailed out of bounds. Their coach shook his head, then clapped his hands and rooted on his players. "Defense! Arms out!"

Jordan again looked back at the bleachers. His parents, Sierra, and Ashley had been joined by Antonio, who waved at Jordan with a churro in his paw.

They're watching me. Jordan groaned inwardly. He raised his injured hand and offered a weak smile. His heart raced when Sierra waved in return.

The Patriots scored again, then again. Near the end of the third quarter, they took the lead: 31–30. It stayed that way for several minutes until a Falcons player was fouled. He made one of two at the line, tying the game.

Jordan buried his face in the towel. He was nervous for his teammates, scared even. He stood up when Manuel took a pass, set his feet, and eyed the rim. Manuel shot the ball in a high arc. It went in! The Patriots were up again: 33–31.

The game went back and forth after that, with neither team leading for long by more than one or two points. By the middle of the fourth quarter, the Patriots starters were visibly tired.

"Jordan!" Coach yelled.

Jordan rose to his feet and stripped off his sweatshirt. He looked into the bleachers one more time. His mom, Antonio, Sierra, and Ashley were all shouting and pumping their fists in the air.

Here I go, he told himself. Then he turned and ran onto the court.

16

EXCEPT FOR THE LAMP on the chest of drawers, the room was dark. Jordan rested on his bed, in clean sweats and a T-shirt, holding his new phone. When he tapped it, a photo of Antonio's face appeared.

"What the heck?" Jordan could see what looked to be sugar crystals in the corners of Antonio's mouth, likely from the churro he'd been eating. He pictured Antonio offering a bite to the others in the bleachers—first to his mom, then to Sierra, then to Ashley.

When his phone was delivered that afternoon, his mother had decided to take it to the game. After all, Jordan had been anxious for its arrival, almost directionless without it. But his mom hadn't given it to him until he got home.

He scrolled to the next image—his mom with sugar crystals at the corners of her mouth. *Really,* Mom? You took a bite of Antonio's churro? He momentarily lowered his head, embarrassed.

He scrolled again: his mom laughing, his mom applauding, his mom scratching her nose, peeling sugar crystals from the corners of her mouth, making a funny face.

And then there was an image of Sierra, looking directly at the phone's camera lens. Her face was serious, yet not serious—*deep* was the word that came to his mind. She was staring intently, as if right at him. She had the look of someone about to ask a serious question.

"Sierra," Jordan cried aloud, his head falling onto the pillow. He was weak with love—what else could it be? Dinner had been a huge plate of spaghetti with meatballs, not leftover enchiladas, after all. So it couldn't be lack of food.

He placed his phone screen down on his chest. *Can she hear my heart?* he wondered. He closed his eyes and tried to imagine what she was doing this very second. Was she on the phone with Ashley? Talking to another friend? Or scrolling through photos? Was there an image of him, Jordan, making the shot that clinched the Patriots' victory over the Falcons?

That had been late in the fourth quarter, only thirteen seconds left on the clock. The Patriots had possession near the basket with a chance to score, but a Falcon player knocked the ball out of Ryan's hands. With sweat stinging his eyes, Jordan had scooped up the ball, went in for the layup, and leapt into the air. His shot kissed the backboard . . . and went in.

"Oh, Sierra," he moaned, closing his eyes. "You are like the Sierra Nevada—majestic in any season." Then he grimaced—that was lame. He would have to come up with another way to describe her beauty. He was continuing to investigate his poetic side when he felt a touch on his arm, and then his fingers. In the world inside his head, it was Sierra touching his hand—yes, touching it tenderly. Then he felt a tongue licking his fingers.

He giggled and sat up. Benny was staring at him, as adorable as any calendar photo, the tip of his red tongue protruding from his mouth.

"You little dude!" Jordan picked up the squirming puppy and hugged him. "You're the coolest canine *en el barrio*."

Jordan left the bedroom holding Benny. Now he understood why people liked dogs so much—they were great.

"Hey, Dad," Jordan said to his father, who was in his recliner as usual, TV muted. On his lap slept Frances.

Mr. Mendoza lifted a finger to his lips and exhaled, "Shhhh."

Jordan sank down onto the couch, gently spilling Benny to the floor.

"How was work?" Jordan asked quietly.

"Same ole, same ole," his dad whispered. He grinned at his son. "I'm glad I got off early. You played great." He described Jordan's last-second shot like a TV announcer, detailing how he had outmaneuvered a Falcon player, then flew over him for the layup.

"Luck," Jordan countered.

"Luck? No way—athletic skill. You soared over that guy.

"Dad, I soared over him because he was the smallest player on their team."

Mr. Mendoza stroked his chin. "OK, I can live with what you're saying." Then he pounded the arm of his recliner, startling Frances, and roared, "But, hey, you scored the winning basket! That's my son!"

"Thanks, Dad. But Ryan was brilliant."

Ryan had scored over half of the team's points.

"Yeah, he was good, the team was good, you were good, and, hey, your phone arrived. Life's good, *qué no*?" He made soft barking sounds at Frances, then cooed, "Did big daddy wake you up? He is so, so sorry."

With his free hand, Mr. Mendoza signaled that he wanted a look at the new phone.

Jordan handed it over.

"Nice," his dad said, nodding. "And cheap, I hope."

"I think so."

At his father's touch, the phone glowed with the photo he'd been looking at.

"What do we have here?" his father asked, smiling. "Is this the girl you were whimpering about?"

"What girl?"

Mr. Mendoza looked up. "What girl? You know what girl. I was sitting next to her—no, she was sitting next to Mom." He chuckled and handed the phone back to Jordan.

Jordan could see that his dad wanted to ask him about Sierra.

"What was her name again?"

Jordan hesitated, then confessed. "Sierra."

"Sierra," his dad said softly. "Like the mountains." He picked up a water glass from the end table, rattled the nearly melted ice cubes, then chugged the remaining liquid. He smiled at Jordan. "So you like her?"

Jordan nodded.

"A lot?"

Jordan nodded again, then admitted, "She doesn't really know me."

"But, hey, she's in your phone—isn't that right?'

At that moment, the phone in his hand chimed and lit up. *Antonio*, Jordan thought in anticipation. But it was not Antonio. The text was from Sierra: "You played unbelievably GREAT. Your mom is GREAT. And the puppies are so CUTE!"

Jordan's dad drummed his thick fingers on the arms of the recliner. He reached for the water glass again, saw that nothing but ice cubes remained, then put it back down. "Who's it from?"

"Sierra."

"What a coincidence." Mr. Mendoza tried to hide his smile. "I wonder if she needs help with her homework?"

Jordan's phone lit up again. This time it was Antonio calling.

"Hey, man," Antonio began as Jordan made for his bedroom. Benny and Frances tried to follow him, but his mother, in the hallway, intercepted them.

"You little stinkers," she sang. She bent down and picked up both dogs. "Boy, you guys are growing!"

Jordan closed his bedroom door behind him. "Guess what?" he asked.

"Like, man, I'm so stuffed my brain don't work good," said Antonio. "What did you have for dinner?"

"Forget dinner! Listen to me. Sierra texted me—what should I do?"

"Like, duh, text her back."

"She said that I played great."

"Well, we know that's a lie." Antonio laughed. "Actually," he continued, in a more serious voice, "you were the gear of all gears."

"The gear of all gears? What does that mean?"

"I don't know. Like I said, I grubbed so much dinner that my brain ain't working good. You ever have that feeling?"

He's impossible! Jordan growled inwardly. He really

wanted to talk about Sierra, to ask if her text meant something other than mere congratulations.

"But honestly," Antonio went on, "that basket gave you hero status." That moment, he told Jordan, had erased his earlier failure on the court. "People will be buying you potato chips all week."

"But tomorrow's Friday."

"That's right, it is, huh?" Antonio then asked Jordan to wait—his mom was calling. A minute later he was back.

"I got to go. My mom's serving dessert." Antonio hung up with a goodbye.

Jordan let his phone slide from his fingers onto his bed. He said good night to his parents, brushed his teeth, then examined his face in the mirror. There was a bruise on his throat—an elbow from an opponent during the scramble for the ball. "Yeah," he said to the mirror, "maybe I am a hero."

He went to bed, suddenly exhausted. Maybe sleep would come with a new dream. Dreams, he'd discovered, could be far better than the real world of a thirteen-year-old boy.

17

IN THE DREAM, Jordan and Sierra were again seated on a 49ers blanket on the bank of the canal.

"Have you ever done anything bad?" Sierra asked.

"Anything bad?" Jordan smiled. "Sierra, I'm thirteen. Of course I have."

"Like what?"

Jordan thought for a moment. He had stolen a Tootsie Roll at a convenience store. He had littered, talked back to a teacher once, and written his name in wet cement. Would admitting to any of those infractions rank as *bad*? Then an idea popped into his head.

"I broke a girl's heart one time."

"You didn't! You're awful."

"It took her a whole year to get over it."

"Brat!"

Jordan giggled, then confessed that this was a lie. He looked longingly at Sierra, whose hair was blowing in the autumn wind. He uttered her name as sweetly as he could.

"Yes, Jordan," said Sierra. "Is this about the heroic layup that won the game?"

"No." Jordan hesitated. "On a scale of one to ten, how handsome am I?"

Sierra stood up. She looked in the direction of the canal, then at the shrubs littered with debris, and finally back at Jordan. "A four."

Jordan leapt to his feet. "A *four*? That good?" He spun in a circle and cried, "The girl says I'm a four!"

Sierra spun with him, then stopped, saying she was dizzy. She pulled her long hair away from her face. "Actually . . ."

"Actually what?"

"Actually you're a nine."

Jordan plopped himself back onto the blanket. He stared at the blue sky.

"A nine and a half," continued Sierra, sitting down next to him, "on the way to becoming a ten."

At that, Jordan turned his face toward hers . . . until something poked him under the chin. He sat up, looking about groggily. The face in front of him belonged to Frances.

"Frances, what are you doing here? You're supposed to be asleep." He took the pup's snout in his hand and gave it a couple of gentle shakes. "Do you know you just destroyed the best dream ever?" He pushed himself into a sitting position and looked around his bedroom. Morning light crept through the blinds. He looked at the clock on his chest of drawers—6:45. He heard his mother in the kitchen and smelled something delicious. He hopped out of bed.

"*Buenas dias, mi* hero," said Mrs. Mendoza as Jordan entered the kitchen.

"Smells awesome," Jordan said, taking a seat at the kitchen table. *No cold cereal this morning*, he thought. He looked at his phone and reread Sierra's text.

"How did you sleep?"

"Great. I had an awesome dream."

His mom lifted her eyebrows, hoping to hear more.

"It was about . . . school."

"School? That's it? Just school?" Wearing an oven mitt over one hand, she presented Jordan with a steaming plate of *chorizo con huevos* with fried weenies on the side, along with a dish towel holding two warm tortillas.

"Mom," he asked, "how does Sierra know my phone number?" Jordan blew on the steaming eggs, then stabbed a circle of weenie.

Mrs. Mendoza sat down at the table. "I gave it to her. And what do you say?"

"Thank you."

"And we're friends now," his mom added.

"What do you mean?" Jordan tore off a piece of tortilla and scooped up some *huevos*.

"We're on Instagram together, ain't we."

"*No me digas!*" Jordan screamed, in imitation of his

father. This was his dad's favorite phrase, after *¿Entiendes, Mendez?*

"Isn't that nice that we're friends?"

His mom and Sierra together on social media! Wasn't there a law against a mom befriending the girl of your dreams? Was there no privacy in a thirteen-year-old's life?

"MOM!"

"Are you OK?" his mom asked innocently. "Did you burn your tongue?"

18

JORDAN ATE his breakfast, sat quietly in the car, then prepared to get out a block from school—their regular routine. He unbuckled his seat belt.

"Wait a second, hero boy," Mrs. Mendoza said. She touched his cheek, played with his hair. "You're so *guapo*," she gushed, pressing two dollars into his palm for an after-school bag of potato chips.

Jordan said, "You're the best," and hurried across the street to a waiting Antonio.

"Hey," Antonio said. "Everyone's talkin' 'bout you." They walked side by side across the front lawn shiny with dew, then headed up the steps of Main Hall.

"You guys are going to the championships next week!" Antonio continued. "Like, awesome! *That* will be a reason to dress up."

Jordan had gotten a text from Coach while in the car. There would be practice on Saturday at ten in the morning.

Antonio placed a hand on Jordan's arm. "Listen, I got something serious to tell you."

"Seriously," replied Jordan, wary of his friend's usual teasing, "are you serious?"

"It's no joke, bro."

"Tell me then."

Antonio gazed over Jordan's shoulder nervously. "Nah, not now—at morning break." He skipped up the steps, leaving Jordan bewildered. Antonio had been a blabbermouth his whole life, unable to keep a secret. Once, when they were six, he told his mom that he and Jordan had been playing with matches, after they had sworn to each other that they wouldn't tell anyone—ever. "Ever" had only lasted about twenty minutes. And when Jordan's mom found out, all hell broke loose.

In language arts class, Jordan found three bags of potato chips on his desk. He looked around at his classmates.

"You did good," the girl next to him said. She pointed at one of the bags. "The lemon-flavored fiery ones are from me."

"Thanks," said Jordan. And he meant it. Antonio had told him that his classmates would hook him up with chips. Now here it was, actually happening—evidence that his friend was not all talk. He stuffed the treats into his backpack.

Mrs. Roosevelt came into the classroom. She beamed at Jordan but didn't say a word about yesterday's game. Instead, she asked the students to fire up their laptops.

"Let's start with a poem I saw on the internet," she

announced. "It's called 'Rumors.'"

A few students moaned—a poem at 9:15 in the morning? Really? To some, poetry was the sort of thing you read at night when you wanted to fall asleep.

"Don't be like that!" Mrs. Roosevelt ordered. "Come on—get on this site." She told them the web address, then asked for a volunteer to read the poem. No one looked up, no one spoke up, and no one raised a hand.

"OK then." Mrs. Roosevelt sat behind her desk, squinted at the screen, then wet her lips and began to read.

Rumors

They say love makes you speechless,
That it takes your breath away,

And right now, as you round
The corner in the hallway,

I, who was telling a friend about the F chord
On a guitar, become speechless.

You pass, and I double over,
Like when, in first grade, Marc Steinberg

Hit me in the stomach
And took my breath away.

When Mrs. Roosevelt finished, she closed the lid of her laptop, smiling. One of her front teeth was streaked with lipstick, and her hair was a little mussed, as if reading the poem had been a wild adventure. She scanned the class. "Let's hear your opinions. What is this poem about?"

When again no one spoke up, Mrs. Roosevelt began to talk—and she went on for the entire class period. Jordan couldn't wait for break, so that he could open the first of many bags of potato chips.

But the poem did make him wonder: *Was love like getting hit in the stomach?* He swallowed hard. That's how it was with him. Sierra *did* take his breath away. No wonder so many love songs were about pain.

Poetry, he had discovered, could be a cool thing.

"Man, we, like, read this poem that I thought was gonna be boring," Jordan began.

"But it wasn't, huh?" Antonio interrupted.

"Nah, I kinda liked it." Jordan offered the bag of chili-lemon potato chips to Antonio. The two were sitting on a splintery bench near the baseball field.

"What was it called?"

"I don't remember," Jordan admitted. "But it was about

this boy being hit by beauty."

"Was it a head punch or a stomach punch?"

"Both. Poor dude." Jordan stuffed a handful of potato chips into his open mouth.

"MAN, I know that poem!" Antonio screamed. "It's dope!" When a potato chip fell from his hand to the ground, he crushed it with his shoe.

"You do?" asked Jordan.

"Nah," Antonio admitted. "I don't know that poem or any poem." He laughed, exposing the mashed potato chips in his mouth. Then he said again, "I got to tell you something."

Jordan blinked at his friend. The blink said, *Yeah, what?*

"I don't want you to laugh—OK?" Antonio warned. "Because, like, I know I sometimes laugh at your stuff—and I'm sorry, like for reals. But this is serious." Antonio paused, waiting for Jordan to respond.

"Promise—I won't laugh."

They bumped fists.

"Like, OK." Antonio took a deep breath and announced, "I play the piccolo."

Jordan wasn't sure what he'd heard. Did Antonio just tell him he played with pickles? Or was there a video game called *Pickle-O?*

"I can see you don't know what a piccolo is. I can tell."

"OK. Like, what is it?"

"A musical instrument."

Jordan absorbed this fact. "A musical instrument? You don't play a musical instrument."

"It's like a flute. And, yeah, I play one—don't laugh."

"A flute. You play the flute?" Jordan dropped his nearly empty bag of potato chips. His best friend played the flute? When did this happen?

"No, no, no. I play the piccolo. It's like a flute but way smaller, and it's made of wood, mostly." He warned Jordan not to tell anybody else.

"I promise. But, like, dang—that's weird. The piccolo . . . really?"

"Yeah, for reals."

It was only a matter of time, he told Jordan, before everyone found out. It was all his mom's fault. She had offered to order him the bike of his dreams if he would take up a musical instrument. Antonio showed Jordan an image of the bike on his phone.

"That's hecka sweet," Jordan crowed.

"Costs like a thousand dollars."

"A thousand dollars!" Jordan screamed. "Man, I would learn the tuba for a bike like that."

"Mom took me down to this pawnshop on Tulare Street."

Jordan could picture that pawnshop. His dad had bought his mom a set of silver spoons and forks from there, plus an antique clock that bonged on the hour.

"But the only instrument they had—except two accordions and a little kid's guitar—was a piccolo. Oh yeah, they had a banjo too, but, like, no way." Antonio sighed and grimaced. "Man, I should have chosen the guitar because . . ." His voice faded.

"Because why?"

Antonio shook his head and clicked his tongue. "Because I got pretty good at playing the piccolo, and now I'm in the pep band."

"The pep band?" Jordan repeated. "We have one of those?"

"It's new. Mr. Peterson's been recruiting members. In fact . . ."

"In fact what?"

"I'll tell you later."

"Tell me now!"

"Nah, you'll see."

The bell rang. Morning break was over. They got up from the splintery bench and started to walk back to class.

Jordan had known Antonio since they were six. If Jordan lost a baby tooth, Antonio lost a baby tooth. If Antonio scraped his knees by falling off his trike, Jordan dutifully fell off his own trike. If Antonio ate frijoles, Jordan ate frijoles. They were like peanut butter and jelly—always together. Now Antonio had surprised him. The *piccolo*?

"But I can tell you this," Antonio began.

"What?"

"Sierra's in the new band too."

"She is?" Jordan's eyes grew wide, then relaxed to their usual size. He wasn't really surprised. "What does she play?"

"The glockenspiel."

"The WHAT?" To Jordan, the unfamiliar word sounded like a bad illness.

But Antonio was already hustling away, jogging backward. "Look it up, bro. Gotta go!"

19

FOR THE REST OF THE MORNING,

Jordan debated whether or not to take up a musical instrument. He considered the guitar, then realized that there were no guitars in a pep band. The same with the piano. The tuba? He couldn't imagine carrying it back and forth to school.

He needed an instrument he could learn fast—in a day or two at most. Then he remembered his dad's harmonica. Were there harmonicas in a pep band? Probably not, he concluded, while secretly devouring a bag of chips in his social studies class. How about the bass drum, the kind found in marching bands? That had to be easy to learn to play.

At lunch break, Jordan pulled on Antonio's sweatshirt. "I got to talk to you."

Antonio was standing with Ashley, Sierra's best friend, on the steps of the library. He immediately began to protest. "But I'm like—"

Just then Sierra emerged from the library, an apple in her hand. She was beaming.

"Here," she said, placing the apple in Jordan's palm.

"You were awesome."

"I was?" Jordan mumbled weakly. He examined the apple as if he had never seen one before.

"That final basket! Everyone went crazy! My heart was really beating."

"It's true," Ashley chimed in, jumping and down. "She was so excited." Ashley waved a hand in front of her face, as if trying to cool herself off.

When a noisy horde of sixth graders began to climb the steps, the four of them meandered in the direction of the cafeteria.

"And your mom," Sierra said, "she's great."

"Jordan's mom?" Antonio interrupted. "She makes the best grub ever. Like she reinvented *huevos con weenies* in a special way. To die for."

Huevos con weenies! *Really, Antonio,* Jordan thought, *do you have to?*

Sierra and Antonio went on discussing Jordan's mother until Jordan, sensing that he was becoming a minor character in his own love story, finally spoke up.

"Glockenspiel," he said.

Sierra tilted her face at him. *What?*

"Why did I say that?" Jordan squeaked. He shrugged. "It just came out."

"He does that a lot," Antonio remarked. "He'll say things that don't make a whole lot of sense, but later you realize—man, that's so wise."

"I do?" Jordan asked.

"Yeah, you do. Like yesterday . . ." Antonio struggled to complete this thought. "Yeah, you said 'chrome ball bearings.' I told him, WHAT? Then later I realized he was thinking how the world runs on chrome ball bearings." He pointed a thumb at Jordan. "This dude can be secretly smart, you know. Feel what I mean?"

Again, Sierra tilted her head. "Yeah," she said. "I think so."

Jordan smiled. His friend had come to his rescue. Peering down at the apple, he said, "Thank you." Then he looked up and, tossing and catching the fruit, remarked, "An apple a day keeps the doctor away."

No one replied. Jordan closed his eyes in embarrassment. *Why did I say that?*

"Hey, what did I tell you?" Antonio shouted. "The guy, he just comes out with these things. That's why he's getting a C in English. Know what I mean?"

All four laughed. Then Ashley chimed in, "Yeah, Jordan, you were awesome on the court."

"Thank you," he said again and lowered his gaze, slightly embarrassed.

"Man, you just be lucky!" Antonio hollered.

Jordan stared at his friend—*stop it*, his gaze warned.

"Nah, man, I'm just kidding. Man, you, like, torched

that other team. What you score—three points?"

Jordan wished that a huge pterodactyl would descend and carry Antonio away. To change the subject, he turned to Sierra. "So you play the glockenspiel?"

"Actually," she replied, "I play the piano—that's my real instrument. But for the band, the one Mr. Peterson is forming—the glockenspiel."

Jordan liked how she said the name of the instrument. It sounded exotic, like the language of a country that had yet to be invented.

"I'd like to hear it."

Sierra looked at Ashley, then at Antonio, and then at Jordan. She was smiling. "You will."

"I will?" Jordan asked.

"We'll be playing at the championship game. That's the band's debut."

Jordan's smile faded, like an ice cube slowly melting. He could imagine the pep band on the sidelines, playing whatever it was they played to boost team morale. Which meant Antonio would be there too. Ever-present Antonio! He searched the sky. Where was that pterodactyl?

"Enjoy your apple," Sierra said, then turned away, hooking Ashley's arm in hers. Jordan watched as they headed off to the cafeteria. When Sierra looked back, she raised one hand and wiggled her fingers at Jordan.

"That was a close one," Antonio said, running a hand over his forehead, as if dispatching sweat. "Once again I had to come to your emotional rescue."

"I can take care of myself."

"You think so, but you need someone like me."

Jordan playfully pushed Antonio. "And what did you mean about that 'chrome ball bearing' thing—where did you get that anyhow?"

"WHERE? Does my bro have to ask?"

"Yeah, I have to ask."

Antonio tapped his forehead. "Here. It's called genius. And it ain't got nothing to do with books." He laughed, wheeled around, then jogged off, pulling up the back of his pants.

Jordan's sudden aloneness felt good. He walked to the front of the campus, to the lawn where couples sometimes strolled, hand in hand. No one was there at the moment.

Sierra, he thought. *Oh, Sierra.* A month ago he would not have acted so pathetically, he told himself. But now he was living the very poem Mrs. Roosevelt had read to the class. He felt punched, right in the stomach. He had lost his breath and lost his senses. He was in love, crazy love.

He tilted his head skyward, ready to burst into song if he could only think of some words. When his gaze returned to ground level, his eyes latched onto a discarded chip bag, filled with wind and sailing across the lawn like some brightly colored bird. In his present state, even litter seemed beautiful.

During the afternoon, Jordan had time to think about Antonio's actions. He confronted his friend after classes had ended for the day.

"Like, I said I was sorry," Antonio said as the two left the school grounds.

"But how come you just didn't disappear?"

"Disappear? I was there to protect you."

"Protect me?"

"Protect you from saying something stupid. What was that thing about an apple a day?"

Jordan shrugged. Maybe his friend had a point.

Antonio continued his explanation. He had to play the role of fool, he argued, so that he—Jordan—wouldn't have to. "Alone," he went on, "you might have blabbered, 'Sierra, I love you more than Romeo dug Juliet.'"

Jordan gulped. He *had* considered making this comparison—if he ever got the opportunity to be alone with her.

"If you do that, you might scare her away for good. Then what?"

Antonio had a point.

"Yeah," Jordan said aloud. "I get it." He sighed and pushed both hands into the front pocket of his hoodie. The apple was there—the apple that Sierra had given him. He would never eat it. He would put it on the chest of drawers in his bedroom and admire it whenever he wasn't playing video games.

"Little dudes," Jordan called as he entered the back door of his house. Benny and Frances had emptied the laundry basket and were pulling on his freshly washed basketball jersey.

The pups abandoned the jersey and raced toward him. Jordan was touched. When was the last time someone had raced toward him? He picked up his jersey, refolded it, then returned it to the basket near the closet.

"Mom?"

Mrs. Mendoza came into the kitchen wearing the pair of rubber gloves she used when cleaning the hallway bathroom. Her hair was out of place and her eyes red from the sting of bathroom cleanser. She stopped, scowled at the pile of laundry, and shook a finger in fake anger at the puppies. "You little rascals." Then she turned to Jordan. "How was school?"

"Pretty good. I have practice tomorrow." He took the bucket of cleaning products from his mom and opened up the door of the closet.

"I know practice makes perfect, but don't hurt yourself."

Jordan shrugged. "I promise I won't." He placed the cleaning products back on the shelf, then asked about his father's old harmonica.

"Harmonica?" responded his mother. "Why?" She took a step toward the closet and inspected herself in the full-length mirror attached to the door. "Boy, I'm a mess."

"Because . . ." Jordan paused. Then he told his mom about Antonio joining the pep band.

"Antonio? Our Antonio?" She shut the closet door and bent down to pick up Frances. She bounced the pup in her arms. "Our funny Antonio can play an instrument? Did you hear that?" she asked Frances, who gave her face a lick.

"Yeah," said Jordan, "the piccolo."

"The piccolo," his mom told the pup. "Antonio plays the piccolo." She was impressed. To Jordan, she said, "Put your clothes away—and nice, OK?" She set Frances down. "You're getting to be a big girl. Soon you'll be dating a big bulldog." She laughed, and then, hands on her hips, eyes squinting, cried, *"Piccolo?"*

Just then Benny pranced up to Jordan, who took him in his arms. His mom fell silent, then began to pet the puppy too.

"Go—put your clothes away," his mom finally said. "And ask Dad about the harmonica when he comes home."

As he was putting his clothes away, Jordan polished the apple from Sierra with one of his clean socks. Then he placed it on top of his chest of drawers, like a trophy.

20

"HERE," SAID MR. MENDOZA as he entered the living room. He was holding out a harmonica. "Why do you want it?"

"It's hard to explain."

Jordan's father plopped down into his recliner, causing the bottom cushion to emit a long, loud sigh. "Hard to explain? What, am I thick in the head?"

Jordan paused before breaking the news, then began, "Did Mom tell you that Antonio plays the piccolo?"

"She did. And I didn't believe her."

"But he does—and he's in the pep band. We're not supposed to say anything to anyone. He's kinda shy about it."

"Antonio, shy? Yeah, right." He chuckled as Frances climbed onto his stomach. "And your school has a pep band?"

Jordan nodded.

"And you want to join the pep band?"

"Maybe."

"Because of this girl."

"Dad, you are totally wrong. She's, like, *the* girl! And, yeah, she's in the band. She plays the glockenspiel."

"Excuse me?" His father smiled. "Are you cussing at your *papi* in German?" He laughed, bouncing the puppy up and down.

"No, Dad, it's an instrument. I looked it up. It sounds like doorbells ringing."

"You're lookin' to play harmonica in the band?"

"Dad, you're smart—you get what I want."

"But, you know," said Mr. Mendoza, pausing when Benny came into the living room. He slapped his knee. "Come here, boy."

Benny, tail wagging, approached the recliner.

"A harmonica," Jordan's dad continued, "is not usually part of a pep band. It's more found in a blues band."

Jordan recognized that this might be a problem. Still, he wanted to learn an instrument. He could imagine starting a band so fresh that listeners from all parts of the globe would check them out on Spotify. Sierra on glockenspiel, Jordan on harmonica, and Antonio on piccolo—a totally new sound. He began to wonder, *Does Ashley play a musical instrument?*

Jordan's phone buzzed: a text from Sierra. He stood up. "Dad," he said. "I got to answer this."

Mr. Mendoza raised his eyebrows so high they nearly touched his hairline. "Let me guess—Sierra? Ask her how her glockenspiel is doing today."

Jordan ignored his father and sprinted to his bedroom,

with Benny and Frances following with their sloppy puppy steps. But he closed the door on them. He needed absolute privacy. Heart racing, he read the text: "Hey, you want to do volunteer work tomorrow?" She had added an emoji: a yellow smiling face. He texted right back: "I got basketball practice. What kind of volunteer work, when and where?"

He stared at his phone, half listening to the sounds of Benny and Frances scratching outside his door. Her response was quick: "Litter cleanup at the canal on McKinley Street. We start at 10:00."

The canal?

He wrote back. "Where exactly at the canal?"

"Near the donut shop."

"I'll be there after practice."

A knock sounded on the bedroom door. When his dad showed his face, Jordan automatically turned his phone screen down.

"What, Dad?"

"I just got a call from work—they need me for an emergency." He frowned and growled. "I'll be gone for a bit. Mom wants to talk to you." He scanned Jordan's bedroom. "You know," he suggested, "this cave could use an airing."

Jordan opened a window, then went to see what his mom wanted. As he entered the kitchen, he noticed that she was finishing up an apple that looked just like the one Sierra had given him.

Jordan tried to hide the shock in his face. *Be cool*, he told himself, *you could be wrong*. He sat down at the kitchen table. *Maybe*, he thought, *it's just an apple from the fruit bowl*.

"I was thinking," said his mom, disposing of the apple core in a small green bin near the back door. "Where to begin?" she continued, wiping her hands on her jeans. "OK, here's what I'm thinking."

Jordan's eyes were on the fruit bowl—a bunch of bananas, two avocados, but no apples.

"You know Sierra?"

"Mom, you know I do."

"I'm thinking because she lost her dog that . . ." Here Mrs. Mendoza paused for a moment, rustling her hair with the tips of her fingers. "That we give one of our puppies to her." She touched Jordan's hand. "Is it still hurting?"

Jordan's mother looked into his face for a response. "What do you think? We'll still have one. And she's such a nice girl."

At that moment Benny and Frances raced into the kitchen. They skidded over the slick floor and tumbled on their sides. Then they righted themselves and began to sniff Jordan's leg.

"I guess so," Jordan said slowly, trying to appear solemn. This was working out better than he could have imagined.

His mother sighed and considered the puppies, who

were now wrestling under the table. "I guess it'll be Benny."

Jordan pouted and said, "Frances, we'll miss you."

The two of them looked stubbornly at each other.

"Benny," Mrs. Mendoza argued.

"Frances," Jordan countered, but not too loudly.

"Benny."

"Frances."

They flipped a quarter. To Jordan's disappointment, Benny would have to go.

"That's settled, then. Sierra—she's such a nice girl. She'll take good care of Benny." Mrs. Mendoza left the room, with both dogs following.

Jordan's phone rang—Antonio.

"Hey, dude, Guess what?"

"Your bike came."

"Man, you like ruined the surprise. But, yeah, it came. We should go for a ride tomorrow."

"I got basketball practice."

"That's right," said Antonio, then he asked if Jordan would like to hear what a piccolo sounded like.

"Sure, I like music."

Jordan listened to an unpleasant roaring sound for thirty seconds.

"That's the piccolo?" Jordan asked, after the roaring stopped.

"Nah, bro, that was the hair dryer. I had to pretty

myself up for this private phone concert."

Antonio began to play the piccolo. Jordan listened and thought, *My bro's got talent*. Then he hung up and headed off to bed.

And the apple from Sierra on his chest of drawers? His mom had eaten it.

21

IN THE DREAM, Jordan pointed at an apple tree hung with fruit.

"Look," sang Sierra. "Strawberries—and a peach tree! I didn't know that peaches grew in November!"

They were at the canal along with thirty other volunteers from school. But the bags they carried were filled not with litter but with ripe fruit of all kinds. There were melons and plums, bunches of red and green grapes, and sweet, fragrant pears.

Jordan and Sierra stopped near a man with a blanket draped over his shoulder. A duffel bag lay at his side.

"I know you," Jordan remarked. It was the homeless person, the one he'd met on the day he rescued Frances. "I gave you a banana."

The man held up a spotted banana. "That's right—I still have it. And I have something you missed." He slowly tugged at the blanket, as if demonstrating a magic trick, to reveal a puppy licking its paw. The puppy raised its head. Its tongue was pink, its eyes soft and innocent.

There was a fourth one! Benny and Frances's sibling!

Jordan woke with a startle. He opened his eyes and

looked around his bedroom, which was dark as dark could get. He grabbed his phone from the floor by the bed: 2:17, it glowed, with three new messages, but he didn't check them. Instead he lay back down, hands on his stomach, and wondered if there really could be a fourth puppy. And the dream of him and Sierra at the canal with every conceivable fruit—what was the meaning of that?

He rolled onto his side, then onto his belly. *Sleep*, he told himself, *sleep*.

He woke again at 4:30, with a shudder. This time, he dressed quietly as a ninja, grabbed a banana as he passed through the kitchen, then tiptoed to the back steps where, sockless, he slipped into his shoes. He rode away on his bike, navigating the neighborhood by instinct more than sight.

When a police cruiser began to tail him, he slowed his pace. "Dang," Jordan muttered to himself, looking over his shoulder.

But the cruiser suddenly gunned its engine and took off down the street. There were more urgent matters than a boy riding a bike in the near dark.

It was still dark when he reached the canal. Moonlight rode on the surface on the water. The stars pulsated above. But in an hour the sky would pale in the east and the trees would become lit with the early light of morning.

Jordan left his bike unlocked—there was no one around.

In the dark, he trudged across the sand to the bank. The current was pushing the water westward, where it would feed into a network of smaller canals and eventually be diverted to individual farms.

Jordan followed the canal eastward, to the place where he had found Frances. He passed the homeless man's encampment, and then the place where he had buried the puppy that didn't survive. It seemed like a long time ago.

He moved through the dark shadows of shrubs and ivy, then paused when he saw a car half-submerged in the water. He knew that stolen cars—often stripped of their license plates—were sometimes rolled into the canal, occasionally with a murder victim dead in the passenger seat, or tied up in the trunk. But what if there had been an accident?

He could see his breath, feel the goose bumps rise on his chest and arms. He didn't want to step into that cold water again. *But what if someone's in there*, he thought fearfully. He stripped off his hoodie and placed it and the banana on the bank. Then he waded into the canal, his pants sucking up water, his shoes sending up small bubbles. He shivered and held his left hand high. He didn't want to reinfect it now.

What am I doing? he asked himself. And yet, he swam toward the car. It was a Honda, with a smashed windshield. He grabbed the door handle and hung on—the current was swift here. He peered into the window, one hand shading his eyes. He couldn't see anyone, but he did notice a dark bundle in the driver's seat. When he found the passenger side locked, he worked himself around the car, slowly, because he didn't want to lose his grip and risk drowning. Then his mom and dad would be forced to identify his body at the city morgue.

He managed to maneuver himself to the driver's side. He held on to the door handle, his body almost horizontal from the current. Then, from the pressure of his fingers on the handle, the car door swung open. A black plastic bag floated out, then bobbed downstream. Jordan watched it float away, then turned his attention to the interior of the car.

No dead body, nothing but a Styrofoam ice chest bouncing off the ceiling.

Jordan worked himself back around the waterlogged Honda and struggled to the shore. He rose from the canal, the water falling off him in sheets. When he looked back at the Honda, one end tipped upward and it moved downstream, but not far.

The black plastic bag was no longer in sight. *It was too small to hold a body*, Jordan thought.

The homeless man stood on the bank, his face full of worry.

"You OK, boy? You trying to kill yourself?"

"You mean, like suicide?" Jordan's teeth were chattering. He blew into his cupped hands and jogged in place.

"Yes, that's what I mean."

"No," Jordan replied.

"That's good," the homeless man said. "Because I think you're looking for her." The man plucked a puppy from a plastic grocery bag. "You have one more—a female." The man smiled, his mouth a dark cave. Then he looked down at the banana next to Jordan's hoodie, his eyes alight with happiness. "I think this is mine, correct?"

22

JORDAN RODE with the third puppy in the pocket of his hoodie. He pedaled fast, with the shadow of his bike and body in front of him, as if they were rushing to get home first. To Jordan, the puppy appeared malnourished. She was shivering and let out a faint whimper as he bumped across each pothole.

He threw his bike down in front of the garage and, after kicking off his soggy shoes, entered the house by the back door. The first thing he heard was his mother's frightened voice.

"Where have you been? You're all wet!"

He removed the puppy from his pocket. His mom put her hand first to her mouth, then to her heart.

"What's going on?" she cried. She looked directly at Jordan. "The canal?"

Jordan nodded.

Mr. Mendoza appeared, still in his robe and with a coffee mug in his hand. "You're wet."

"Dad," Jordan said, "there was another one."

Jordan's mother sank down in a chair and covered her eyes with one hand—she was about to cry. His father took the pup into his large workman's hands.

"I can't believe it!" his dad whispered. "*¡No lo creo!* Another one?"

"Jordan," his mother pleaded, eyes brimming with tears. "I don't understand. How?"

Jordan described his dream, still fresh in his memory, how he'd seen the homeless man holding the puppy. It felt as if he had been calling for Jordan to come and get her.

"In your dream?" his mom asked. "You saw this person holding him in your dream?" She looked over at the puppy, who was still shivering.

"Her," Jordan corrected. "I don't know if dreams usually come true, but this one did."

Mrs. Mendoza held her arms out, beckoning for the puppy. "Give her to me," she told her husband. "Jordan, get the formula."

Jordan hurried into the pantry, returning with a can of puppy milk and a clean bottle.

His parents stood side by side, both looking down at this miracle.

"Poor thing." Jordan's mom petted the top of the pup's head and removed a damp leaf from the bottom of a paw.

Jordan opened the can, measured some formula into the bottle, then handed it to his mother, who was once again seated in a chair. The three hovered over the puppy, who, eyes closed, began to nurse.

"She's hungry," Jordan's father said, fingering some debris from one floppy ear. The puppy flinched, stopped nursing, then began again.

"She's so small," Jordan said, judging that she was only half the size of Benny and Frances. The pup had been starving.

The puppy choked for a second but returned immediately to the bottle. She swallowed the few ounces, burped, then looked up at the three of them. She had drunk so enthusiastically that a few drops of milk clung to her eyelashes.

"Just like you, Jordan," his mom said, wiping a tear from the side of her nose. "You were so messy when you nursed."

"I was?"

"No," she laughed. "Actually, you were a proper baby. And now—you're such a brave son."

"*Es la verdad*," his father agreed, squeezing Jordan's shoulder.

Benny and Frances, tails wagging, snouts sniffing, ventured into the kitchen.

"Your sister," Mr. Mendoza announced to the puppies. They looked up momentarily, then turned to sniff at a few fallen drops of milk. They licked the floor clean.

Mr. Mendoza eyed Jordan. "You're still wet."

Jordan gazed down at his pants—the fabric was stuck to his legs.

"Tell me what happened," his father said.

Jordan sneezed. "I'm really cold, Dad. Let me take a shower first."

Dressed in fresh, dry clothes, Jordan joined his parents, who were seated on the living room couch. The puppy was resting between them on a towel, her head turning weakly as she sized up her new home.

Jordan dropped to his knees and petted her.

"OK, now," his father demanded.

"It was in my dreams, like I told you."

"Now your *papi* is supposed to remember your dreams?" He chuckled and ran a hand down his work-tired face. "OK, so what was this dream about?"

"It was about me and my friends at the canal and everything was sort of beautiful, then I woke up, scared." He recalled how, in that moment, he had pictured a fourth puppy—a puppy being kept alive by the homeless man.

"The same man you mentioned before?" his mom asked.

"Yeah, the same one." Then he described waking before dawn and returning to the canal, seeing the Honda submerged in the water, and, for one frightening moment, imagining—wrongly, he told them—that someone was trapped inside.

"When I came out of the water—it was hecka cold—there was the homeless man. He was, like, waiting for me." Jordan pointed at the puppy. "He brought her out of a plastic bag and gave her to me."

"Just handed her over?" his dad inquired.

"Yeah, like he was waiting for me. It was weird 'cause that's what I dreamed."

Neither of his parents spoke up. They stared at him instead, as if he were something new and unusual.

"*Mi'jo*," said his father, "like Mom said, you're really brave. No one was in the car?"

"I checked."

"Yeah," his dad said, cracking a knuckle. "Probably stolen and abandoned. The city's going to the dogs." He laughed, then muttered to himself, "Going to the dogs—that's funny."

"It's so scary." Mrs. Mendoza shuddered. "Jordan, I don't want you to go there no more." She gave him a warning look. "*¿Entiendes?*"

Jordan nodded, saying nothing about Sierra's invitation.

"Let me see your hand," his father said, brow pleated with worry. "*A ver.*"

Jordan turned his hand over several times.

"Looks OK," his dad said. "You taking your penicillin pills?"

"Yeah, I am. Just two more days."

Jordan's mother got up from the couch. "Breakfast," she announced.

Benny and Frances followed his mom into the kitchen. The new puppy closed her eyes and went to sleep with a single drop of milk hanging from her ear.

23

PEDRO SHOWED UP at basketball practice on crutches and carefully sat down in a folding chair.

Jordan greeted him solemnly. "Sorry, man," he said.

The two bumped fists.

"I heard you were the hero," Pedro remarked.

"Hero? Nah, just lucky."

"Lucky's good, bro." He looked down at the cast on his leg. "Me, I had bad luck. No one else got hurt in the crash. Just me. But that's cool."

One after another, the team members greeted Pedro, then took to the court. They did drills for the first half hour, mainly pick-and-rolls, but also layups, inbound passes, and free throws.

Coach Ramirez clapped his hands for the players to stop and gather round. "The Bears," he said, "they're big. They're gonna pretend they got fouled—bunch of actors falling over when you just touch them. Free throws are gonna be important." He scanned his players. "Now," he said, "let's have a friendly match."

To Jordan's surprise, Coach placed him on the A team, with the starters. As the scrimmage went on, he and Ryan began to sync their movements, gaining a better sense of how to play a two-man game on offense. The A team beat the B team 19–8. Ryan scored eight of those points, Manuel six, and Jordan five—two buckets and a single free throw.

After the scrimmage, the players assembled in the bleachers to listen to their coach.

"Like I said," Coach warned, pacing in front of them, "they're gonna be tough. Especially without Pedro."

When everyone clapped, Pedro waved off the praise with a smile.

"They went 7–0 in league play and spanked the Falcons," Coach went on. The Bears, he observed, also had the home advantage because the game would be held at their school. "But, hey," he shouted, "we like competition—don't we?"

Ryan roared, "Bring it on!" Others echoed, "Bring it on!" The whole team went wild and waved their towels over their heads.

"That's what I'm talkin' about!" Coach roared in return, waving his own towel. He reminded them that there would be practice on Monday and Tuesday, then closed with, "And guess what?" He scanned the faces of the players. "We have a pep band."

The players looked confused. "A pep band?" asked Pedro. "What's that?"

Coach made like he was playing the violin. "Music, boys! To fire you up!"

"We're already fired up!" Manuel yelled, and blew an invisible saxophone.

When the team meeting was over, Coach pulled Jordan aside before he had a chance to head to the locker room.

"You're looking good, Mendoza. How's the paw?"

Jordan made a fist, then released it. He sneezed, then said, "OK."

"You ain't coming down with a cold, are you?"

"No," Jordan lied. But he could feel something building in his chest and moving into his sinuses.

Coach eyed Jordan suspiciously. Then he told him to go home and rest up.

"You were awesome!" Antonio crowed. "You're gonna destroy them." He had come to the gym midway through Saturday's practice. From high in the bleachers, he had watched the scrimmage between the A and B teams.

"I'm tired," Jordan replied, hands on his knees.

"What you mean, tired? How can you be tired when you scored all the buckets, huh?"

Jordan stood upright and bumped fists with Antonio. "Don't exaggerate. I scored five points."

"Five? You mean five hundred?"

Jordan flicked his towel at his friend and went off to

shower. Afterward the two headed to the canal. Jordan felt slightly guilty for not heeding Coach's order to rest, but he hoped the volunteers would still be at work on their cleanup project. More than anything, he wanted another opportunity to see Sierra.

When they arrived, they were surprised to find three police cruisers and a white van bearing the words "Crime Scene Lab." A tow truck was quietly rumbling at the edge of the water. In a nearby tree, two little kids were perched on a high branch, making a commotion.

Jordan and Antonio stopped their bikes some distance away, surprised. They watched wordlessly as the police officers patrolled the bank.

Antonio asked, "Think someone drowned?"

Jordan closed his eyes and tried to picture a boy his age, floating facedown in the water. He shrugged and said, "Nah, I don't think so."

They pushed their bikes closer. As they approached, a cop eyed them. His stare said, *Don't come any closer.*

Jordan didn't see any volunteers from school. The cleanup had been canceled, he suspected. Then he spotted the waterlogged Honda. It had been pulled from the canal. Both doors were open, along with the trunk.

Jordan turned to Antonio. "I got to tell you something," he began. Then he briefly described last night's dream and the morning's rescue.

"Really?" Antonio asked.

"Yeah, really. The homeless guy was there, like in the dream. And he gave me the puppy. Brought it right out of a plastic bag."

Antonio studied Jordan's face. "You're telling the truth, huh?"

Then Jordan described swimming out to the Honda to check if someone was trapped inside.

"I'm supposed to believe that too?"

"It's true."

Antonio nodded and sighed from relief that he could believe his friend. "Yeah, you're telling the truth. But, dang, what a story."

The two watched the tow truck hitch up the Honda, then drive slowly away, dripping water as it moved down the street.

"Officer!" Jordan called.

"Don't call him," warned Antonio under his breath. "What's wrong with you?"

Jordan ignored his friend. The officer took a few steps toward the boys.

"I got to ask," he began, "was anyone hurt?"

The officer told them that the Honda had been stolen, then used in a burglary. Drugs—all soggy—had been found in the trunk. The culprits—all in their teens—were safely in jail.

Jordan and Antonio got back on their bikes and started for home. They rode together for several blocks, then separated, promising to hook up later. Jordan's eyes were watering, and he sneezed again. He was definitely coming down with something.

24

WHEN JORDAN GOT HOME, the door was locked. He let himself in with the key the family kept in a flowerpot near the back door. The house was quiet. He searched the living room—no puppies. He poked his nose in his parents' bedroom, then in the third bedroom, used mostly for storage. Still no puppies.

He texted his mom: "Where are you guys?" Then he texted Sierra: "What happened at the canal?"

With his stomach rumbling, he piled three kinds of lunch meat on a slice of bread, placed a couple of potato chips on top, then pressed another slice of bread onto the pile. The chips crackled like bones.

"Who says I can't cook?" he joked to himself.

He was on the last bites of his sandwich when he got a reply from his mom. They were at the veterinarian's office, getting shots for all three pups. But they were also really concerned for the new puppy. She still seemed weak and had vomited after feeding.

Shots? Jordan imagined a long needle pressing into each puppy's hind leg—poor things. That thought reminded him to take a penicillin pill, the next to the last. He flexed his hand and fingers. It hardly hurt at all.

Seconds later Sierra texted him. The cleanup project had been canceled at the last minute because of an active crime scene. She asked him about practice.

I'm on her mind, Jordan thought. He immediately texted her back and suggested that the two of them do a litter patrol on their own, tomorrow, Sunday, if she liked.

He nibbled a cookie while staring at his phone. "Yes that would work," she answered. "2 p.m. and remember to bring gloves and plastic bags."

Time alone with Sierra? Jordan was overjoyed. The cookie crumbs were like sand in his mouth, tasteless. True sweetness was her acceptance of his invitation.

Minutes later, Antonio texted that he was going to join them. "Should I bring anything?" he asked.

What! Angry, Jordan called Antonio, but he didn't pick up. He left a brief message: "Dude, I want to be alone with Sierra—get it?"

Jordan heard his father's truck squeaking up the driveway. Through the front window, he could see that his parents had bought groceries in addition to taking the puppies to the vet. He went outside to help.

His dad handed him the box of puppies. *"Ay,"* he moaned playfully, "a long day on the planet."

Inside, Jordan placed the box on the carpeted floor of the living room, then carefully tipped it sideways. Out rolled the three puppies, who righted themselves and looked around as if they had never seen this place before. But when Jordan lowered himself to his knees, they recognized him immediately. It showed in their wagging tails.

"Did it hurt?" cooed Jordan.

The puppies licked his face and hands. His heart beat in rhythm with their tails. He pulled his phone from his back pocket. "Cheese," he told the puppies, then snapped their picture.

"How was practice?" Mr. Mendoza asked, after putting away the groceries.

Jordan sneezed. "Pretty good," he said, wiping his nose. "Coach is going to start me, I think."

"Are you getting sick?" his mother asked.

"I don't know," Jordan replied. "But listen." He told his parents what Sierra had told him about the canal. "There was, like, crime-scene tape and a police van. Just like in the movies."

"It's crazy out there," Mr. Mendoza said. He lifted up the newest puppy and got comfy in the recliner.

Jordan sneezed again. "Yeah, it is."

"Looks like a cold to me," said his father. He handed Jordan the box of Kleenex from the table next to his chair.

Jordan shrugged and blew his nose. "Nah, it's the puppies. Their fur."

"You guys," his dad said, turning to the puppies, "are

costing me *mucho dinero*." He held the puppy up in the air like a trophy, then hugged her and planted a kiss on her scruff. "Good thing the vet said you were all way healthy."

Mrs. Mendoza stood in front of Jordan and scrutinized his face. "You're sick."

"No I'm not," he replied, plucking another Kleenex from the box.

"Yes you are. You're staying home."

"I didn't do anything wrong. Like, that's so unfair."

"Oh, poor you. I'm your mom. I know. You have a cold." Mrs. Mendoza ordered him to bed.

Jordan stomped off to his bedroom but didn't crawl into bed. He played video games, listened to music, and blew his nose every few minutes.

Then his mother called, "Jordan, *comida* time. Wash your paws."

In the kitchen, Mrs. Mendoza felt his forehead and cheeks and tried to look up his nostrils.

"Mom," said Jordan, almost laughing, "that's too personal." He stifled another sneeze. "Anyway," he continued, "I'm only a little bit sick."

Over a heaping bowl of lemon-flavored noodles, Jordan described the scene at the canal, beginning with the tow truck pulling the Honda from the water, proceeding to a helicopter that nearly crashed into a power line, then adding a SWAT team riding the coolest off-road motorcycles.

Mr. Mendoza, half smiling, lapped up his every word. "How about the National Guard?" he asked, playing along with the story. "Were they called in too?"

"Yeah, a lot of 'em," said Jordan. "They wore like these camouflage uniforms. They were cool."

Jordan's mother got up for a second helping, then returned to the table. She smiled at her son. "Now I really know you're sick. You're delusional."

Antonio called around eight.

"What did you have for dinner?"

"Food."

"Like, duh."

"Macaroni and cheese with pieces of sliced hot dog."

Antonio hesitated a moment before concluding, "That sounds good."

"Forget dinner! Like how come you have to come with us?"

"Bro, listen to yourself. Like, soooo jealous. Sierra invited me."

Impossible. Jordan snarled silently. Antonio and Sierra had been seeing each other almost every day. They were in the pep band together. He asked whether the harmonica was ever part of a pep band.

"The harmonica? I gotta straight-up answer—no, bro."

"Never?"

"Yeah, never, ever. Why?"

"My dad gave me his harmonica."

"That's nice of your daddy-o. But let's stop 'bout the harmonica. Back to Sierra." He told Jordan that he would kick around with them for a while and then, holy guacamole, remember that he had to do something at home. "But I gotta warn you."

Jordan listened.

"Be cool. Don't freak her out. She's nice and stuff."

"Does it show that I like her?"

"Like, it's obvious, dude." He asked what Jordan was going to have for dessert.

"Ice cream."

"What kind?"

"The kind that has like three flavors."

"*Ay, papi*, Neapolitan! Be at your crib in ten minutes!" Antonio hung up.

Jordan knew that his friend wouldn't really come over. After eating his ice cream, he dressed in his pajamas, went into the bathroom to brush his teeth—hard—then petted the puppies good night. They were in a box near the back door. It had been a long day for them, he thought, and they'd had shots. Did they cry from the pain? he wondered.

In his bedroom, he scrolled his phone—nothing spectacular, just a few encouraging words for the team from Coach. He hopped into bed, got comfy, turned off his light, and blinked in the dark.

He hugged his pillow and wondered whether Sierra was as squeezable. He sneezed, coughed, and then was forced to admit the obvious: *I'm sick*. If his parents knew how bad his cold was, they wouldn't let him leave the house tomorrow. Instead, they would order him to bed or to the couch. On the couch he would be forced to do his homework. How much fun would that be on a Sunday when the person you liked was waiting for you? He squeezed his pillow and then fell into a dreamless sleep.

25

JORDAN WOKE COUGHING. He plodded sleepy-eyed to the kitchen, a Kleenex balled up in his hand. He was sick.

His mother was peeling potatoes at the sink. "How do you feel?" she asked.

"Great," he answered, then coughed.

"You're not great!" Mrs. Mendoza put down the potato and wiped her hands on a dish towel. With a worried look, she felt his forehead and patted his cheeks—he wasn't hot. But as a mother, she recognized a sick boy when she saw one.

"Back to bed."

"But Mom."

She jabbed her finger in the direction of his bedroom. "Now!"

Back in bed, Jordan looked at his phone. Sierra had texted, "See you at 2:00." He wrote back: "OK, great! Can't wait!" He lowered his head onto a pillow and closed his eyes. Sierra was there. Her hair was blowing in the wind. Her teeth were sparkling bright. When she pushed her hair away from her face, he saw that her fingernails were painted glossy peach and that she wore a heart-shaped ring. Then, among these images, he saw Antonio eating a churro so huge it could have fed three teenage boys.

Jordan opened his eyes. *My bro*, he thought, *has to ruin it all!* His phone buzzed: a text from Antonio, asking what he'd had for Sunday breakfast. Groaning, he texted a lie: "A bowl of cereal and an old hot dog." Antonio immediately wrote back, "Ah man sounds so good."

Jordan roused himself from bed. He dressed, then went into the bathroom, where he drank some warm water to clear his throat. Then he returned to the kitchen, holding his back straight as a soldier's.

His mom was at the stove. "I told you to stay in bed."

"Bed, Mom, is for sleep. I don't feel sleepy. Where's Dad?"

She pointed a spatula toward the back door. "Boys," she muttered.

She was frying potatoes in a large skillet. A carton of eggs was open on the counter next to her, ready to go. She had already fried a dozen strips of bacon until they were crispy, then laid them out on a large white plate.

Jordan went outside. He slipped into his sneakers and, laces dragging, approached his father, who was seated on a redwood bench, watching the pups play.

"They sure are goofy," his dad said heartily.

Jordan watched the puppies too. "Dad," he said, "Mom thinks I'm sick."

"Sick?" laughed his father. "My son never gets sick. He jumps into canals every other day."

Benny began to pull at Jordan's undone laces, growling. "Seriously, Dad," said Jordan, explaining his plan to meet Sierra that afternoon.

"Sierra?"

"You remember. She plays the glockenspiel."

"Cussing at your *papi* again? No *respeto*."

"Dad, I know you're playing with me. But Mom . . . tell her I'm OK." Jordan sneezed, then blew his nose. He looked at the contents of the Kleenex—frog green.

"Are you sure?" Jordan's father felt his cheek. "Except for your *mocos*, you seem OK."

"Yeah, I feel good—honest." He smiled at the pups, who were chewing away at his laces. He picked up the littlest and held her close to his face. "We still have to name you."

"That's right," said his dad. "I'll think of the names of some old girlfriends. Maybe one will suit this pup." He looked closely at the puppy in Jordan's arms. "She does have Gloria's eyes."

"Dad, don't go there," said Jordan, but he couldn't help himself from asking. "Who's Gloria?"

Mr. Mendoza chuckled. "Never mind," he said.

At breakfast, Jordan's father praised his wife's *chorizo con huevos*, with papas on the side, the crispy bacon, and the tortillas that, though store-bought, were the best in the world. Then he observed that their son, a hero, had never, ever felt better. Her breakfast had healed him completely!

Jordan smiled at his mother. "Dad would never lie," he said, his mouth still filled with food.

Standing in front of the bathroom mirror, Jordan swatted some of his dad's cologne onto his throat. *This*, he considered, *is my first real date.* True, he had liked Tracie, a girl in fifth grade, and they had gone to the mall together. They'd walked from store to store and left without making any purchases. But on the way home, he did buy her a candy bar from a gas station. Still, his mom was with them the whole time, so it didn't count as a date.

But did litter patrol really qualify as a date? He had no immediate answer—and that was fine. For now, he pulled a freshly washed sweatshirt over his head. He checked his wallet—a ten-dollar bill. He sneezed once, then a second time. But no cold would keep him from seeing Sierra. He looked at his phone: 1:35.

Jordan turned the light off in the bathroom and hurried back to his room. He gathered the supplies he'd laid out on the bed: chewing gum, a candy bar to share, pocket-sized hand wipes, Kleenex, his phone . . .

"Where are you going?" his mom asked from his doorway.

"Mom, you know where."

"I do?" she asked playfully. Then continued, "And are you gonna ask her? About Benny?"

"OK, Mom, I'll ask if she—" Jordan was interrupted by a knock on the front door.

His mother left the room to answer it. "Yes?" she asked, opening the door a few inches.

"Mrs. Mendez?" a man in a suit inquired.

"Yes."

"Police detectives, juvenile division. We're here about your son."

"My son?" She looked over her shoulder at Jordan, who had come into the living room.

He held back for a moment, then quietly approached his mother. "About what?"

"Can we talk?" a second man asked. "Outside if you like."

Mrs. Mendoza stepped onto the porch, but not before gesturing for Jordan to get his father.

Jordan hurried to the kitchen, where his dad was seated on a stool, watching a soccer match on the computer.

Jordan whispered, "There's someone at the door."

"Those religious people?"

"No, the police, I think."

Mr. Mendoza slid from the stool and hitched up his pants. He walked to the front door, with Jordan trailing, then looked out onto the porch.

"What's this about?" he asked sternly.

"I'm Detective Anderson," said the man in the suit. "This is Detective Jefferson," he continued, nodding at his partner. His eyes slid to Jordan. "It's about your son."

Mr. Mendoza looked at Jordan. "My son?"

"It regards trouble at the canal on McKinley."

Jordan's father relaxed. "You mean the puppies? Jordan saved them."

"Puppies?" Detective Jefferson asked with a confused expression.

"Yeah, he saved them. Is that what you're talking about?"

"No," Detective Anderson answered. "His fingerprints were found on a stolen car. Drugs were involved."

Mr. Mendoza grimaced, then stepped out in front of his wife, who now had her arm around Jordan's waist.

"I don't understand. My son doesn't steal or do drugs," Mr. Mendoza declared.

Detective Anderson asked if they could question Jordan. His lips were tight, his eyes were dark, his mood serious.

"Go ahead," said Mr. Mendoza, "ask him anything." He placed a supportive hand on Jordan's shoulder.

"Down at juvenile hall."

"Juvenile hall," said Jordan's father, not even trying to hide his scowl. "What's wrong with right here?"

The detective did not reply.

"OK, we'll drive there. Where is it?"

The detectives looked at one another. Detective Jefferson said, "The boy has to come with us. And we need his phone."

"He's a good boy," Mrs. Mendoza said. "Why do you need his phone?"

"We just do," said Detective Jefferson, hand outstretched, palm up.

Jordan gave up his phone. Now how would he tell Sierra he wasn't coming to the canal? The detective turned it over several times in his hands. "Seems new."

"My other phone got ruined."

The two detectives lifted their eyebrows, suggesting that they didn't believe him. "You can tell us all about it later."

The phone suddenly chimed.

"Answer it," ordered Detective Jefferson, staring at the screen. Jordan was anticipating a call from Sierra but, when he tapped the screen, it was Antonio's voice that sounded. "Hey, fool, you with Sierra? I can't go with you. I'm locked down practicing the piccolo. Call me when you all finished."

"Practicing the piccolo?" Detective Anderson repeated.

He cast a glance his partner. "Code words maybe?"

Mr. and Mrs. Mendoza quickly retreated inside, then reemerged wearing their coats.

Jordan's dad waved at the detectives. "Let's go," he said.

26

JORDAN THOUGHT it would be cool to ride in the back of a police cruiser, if only he weren't a suspect. But there he was, buckled up and scared, a hand over his mouth because the back seat smelled of sweat, pee, and what he imagined was vomit. He swiveled his head to see his parents following in their car. *Poor Mom,* he thought, *she looks sad.* And Dad? His face showed a dark anger.

Jordan was placed in a small, windowless room with a single camera, like a large eyeball, near the ceiling. He hunkered there alone, the cologne on his neck washed away by fear. He recalled his father watching the news from his recliner, then braying that life was unfair. Now he understood what that meant. He pictured Sierra at the canal, holding a black trash bag in her gloved hands. She would wait an hour, maybe. She would text him, call him, then call her best friend, Ashley, before returning home, disappointed and super angry. She would pound the sand from her shoes and promise not to bother with Jordan Mendoza—ever again!

The two detectives sauntered into the room. They had removed their coats and neckties and now wore their collars open. Detective Anderson quietly sat down, placing a folder on the table, while Detective Jefferson stood a few feet behind him, arms crossed.

"Your fingerprints were on the door handle," Detective Anderson stated. "Can you explain why?"

"If I tell you," Jordan said, "you won't believe it."

"Nah, Jordan," said Detective Jefferson. "We'll believe what you have to say. We know you're a good kid."

"I know you won't," retorted Jordan, his own arms now across his chest. In fact, Jordan wasn't sure if even he could believe his own story. A seventh-grade boy risking his life to see if anyone was trapped in a sunken car?

"Try us," Detective Anderson suggested.

Jordan lowered his gaze. He sighed, then said, "It's like this." He began by telling the officers about rescuing the first puppy. Then he told about the dream that forced him to return to the canal, where he discovered two more puppies—one dead, one alive. While at the canal that second time, he encountered a homeless man and gave him the banana he was carrying for a snack.

"A banana?" Detective Anderson asked.

"It's true. Like I said, one pup alive and the other dead." Jordan sneezed. "Sorry," he said. "I have a cold."

"I see," Detective Anderson said. "Continue."

"Then I had that second dream—no, maybe it was a third dream. This cold makes it hard to think."

"Second or third dream?" laughed Detective Anderson. He turned to his partner. "This boy is a real dreamer."

Jordan ignored this comment. He explained that he liked this girl, Sierra, a lot—and that in the dream the two of them were at the canal. Only the canal was not filled with trash but beautiful, with fruit trees and grapevines. And there was the homeless man with another puppy under his blanket. Then he had woken up, scared. "And that's when I thought there might be a fourth puppy."

"Let me get this straight," Detective Anderson said, bending a paper clip just like Vice Principal Hollister did. "You rescued a puppy from the canal, had a dream . . ."

"Two or three dreams."

"OK," agreed Detective Anderson, "two or three dreams. Then you go down to the canal again, encounter a homeless guy, give him a banana, take home a second puppy but not the third one because that one's dead. Then another dream spurs you to return to the canal once more, where the homeless guy gives you a fourth puppy." He threw his pencil onto the folder. "Makes perfect sense."

"That's close," said Jordan. "But it's like this, really." He told about riding his bike to the canal on Saturday to search for the fourth puppy and how he'd discovered the submerged car.

"The Honda," Detective Jefferson said.

"Yeah, and, like, I had this crazy idea that maybe

someone was trapped inside." He described how he waded into the water, then swam to the car. "The passenger side was locked, so I went around to the other side and opened the door."

"Thus, your fingerprints?" Detective Anderson scratched his head, then turned to Detective Jefferson. "Seems clear to me."

"Yep," Detective Jefferson added. "Makes perfect sense."

Jordan ignored their sarcasm. "What I'm telling you is the truth. Honest."

"Why the new phone?" Detective Jefferson asked.

"Because the first time—when I saw the puppy in the water—I jumped in with my phone in my pocket. It got ruined."

Detective Anderson flicked the bent paper clip into the corner of the room. "What we have here, Detective Jefferson, is a dreamer with a wild imagination."

"Check my phone," Jordan suggested. "There's pictures of the puppies."

"What are the names of the pups?" asked Detective Jefferson.

"Benny and Frances."

"Benny and Frances." Detective Anderson chuckled. "Good dog names. And the third?"

"We haven't named it yet."

Detective Anderson placed Jordan's phone on the table and scrolled the photos until he locked eyes on the puppies. He showed the phone to Detective Jefferson, who asked, "What are their names again?"

"Benny and Frances."

Detective Jefferson laughed and clapped his NBA-sized hands. "Sounds like a comedy act." He pretended to wipe a tear from his eye. "And this one has no name?"

Jordan shook his head. "It's a female pup," he said.

"In that case," Detective Jefferson said, "may I suggest Fifi?" He chuckled unpleasantly, then launched into a brief history of the Honda's last moments. The car, he explained, had been involved in a drug crime gone wrong.

Jordan recalled the plastic trash bag that had floated away after he'd opened the car door. Were drugs inside? Bundles of hundred-dollar bills? Terrorist codes? Grenades even?

"You *seem* like a good kid," admitted Detective Anderson. He tapped the folder in front of him, then opened it and scanned the contents: a single sheet of paper. "Let's see." He smiled. "C, C, C, C—and an A in physical education."

"Exemplary student," Detective Jefferson concluded.

My report card! How did they get that? wondered Jordan. Had they called the principal on Sunday? Plus, how did they get his fingerprints?

The detectives handed Jordan's phone back and told him he could go, but not before Detective Anderson pointed out that he had two calls from a girl named Sierra and eight from a boy named Antonio.

In the back seat of the family car, Jordan sneezed twice and blew his nose three times.

His father, looming large over the steering wheel, looked angry, but his mother sat calmly in the passenger's seat, checking her phone.

"They treated you like a criminal—*mi hijo!*" his father fumed, occasionally casting his eyes at the rearview mirror, where he could see Jordan in the back seat.

"Dad," Jordan said, "it's OK, really. They found my fingerprints on the door handle." Then he asked how they could have known it was him.

"When we went to Mexico," his mother explained, "we had to go through security." Although he had been only six years old at the time, his fingerprints had been scanned along with everyone else's.

"Really?" Jordan asked. "Then I'm in the system."

"Better there than in juvie," retorted his mom.

"There's no privacy anywhere," grumbled Mr. Mendoza. He pointed out the window, at a corner convenience store. "See—there's a camera now."

"Where?" Jordan asked, peering behind them.

"You missed it," growled his father. Then he added that the government was watching everything—even what you searched for on your computer.

"But you don't do anything online but shop," Jordan countered. "And watch soccer."

"Football, son, football—not soccer." Then he asked what the detectives had questioned him about.

"Mainly why I kept going to the canal to rescue puppies."

"If they had asked me," said his father, "I'd have said it's none of their business. Then stuck my tongue out at them."

"*Ay, hombre*," said Jordan's mother. "It's their job."

"Their job? Bothering good kids?" Mr. Mendoza's fury was building. He pointed out the window again. "Hey, look, another camera!" He smiled and waved.

Jordan tried and failed to spot that camera too, as well as a camera on the next street. But when his father pulled into the driveway, he pointed at the porch and joked, "There's another one." It was their own surveillance camera, mounted under the awning, its lens directed at their own boring street. *What crimes had ever occurred in our neighborhood?* Jordan wondered. Forgetful Mr. Bend sometimes left his sprinkler to run for hours, wasting water that ran into the gutters. Did that count?

"I'm glad we have one," his mother said, unbuckling

her seat belt. "You never know."

They all piled out of the car.

When Mr. Mendoza pushed open the front door, the family was greeted by three puppies prancing in a circle.

"Intruders!" Jordan's father yelled, leveling his hands like pistols. "Call the cops!"

Four o'clock in the afternoon. Jordan sat propped up in bed, wearing pajamas and a robe. He texted Sierra, apologizing for not showing up at the canal. "I had a good reason," he tapped out on his phone. He sent the message and stared at the screen: no response.

Then a text from Antonio arrived. "How was the date? Did you hold her hand? Kiss her? Give her the candy bar to share like you said you would?" His emoji was a wink.

"This is America," Jordan replied. "None of your business." He wrote this as a joke, in imitation of his dad, and expected that his friend would write back immediately. No response.

Jordan picked at his dinner that evening, then shuffled back to his bedroom, growing sicker by the hour. He could tell he wouldn't be able to go to school tomorrow. He sneezed and coughed until his mother came in with a cold towel to wipe his brow.

"Were they mean?" she asked. "The detectives?" Jordan could tell that she hadn't wanted to ask this question in his dad's presence. He would have pounded the arms of his recliner and shouted that they lived in a police state.

"Nah, Mom, they just asked questions."

"I hope they catch the crooks. They ruined someone's nice car." She patted his forehead, then said, "We can give Sierra the littlest puppy. In a week or two, maybe."

"I think she's mad at me."

"Mad? *¿Por que?*"

"You know. Like, I stood her up."

"You explained what happened, didn't you?"

"I did. Or at least I think I did." No matter what the explanation, he could see why she might be mad.

"I could text her—"

Jordan's hands clenched with fear. His mom writing in his defense—never! "No, Mom," he cried. "Please don't even suggest it. It's between me and her. OK?"

Mrs. Mendoza placed her palms against Jordan's cheeks. "You're a little warm. You need to sleep. No more jumping into canals. Promise?"

"Promise," Jordan said, then sneezed again.

After his mother left the bedroom, the next visitor was his dad. Their big dinner seemed to have mellowed him.

"Long day for you," said Mr. Mendoza.

"Super long."

"What do you think of calling the littlest pup Dawn?"

Jordan mulled over the suggestion. "Dawn?" he asked.

"Isn't that the name of a dish soap?"

His father laughed. "Yeah, but it's also the time of day. That was when you found the pup, at daybreak."

"Dawn," Jordan repeated to himself. He shrugged. "Sounds nice." He blew his nose, then asked, "Did you have a girlfriend named Dawn?"

His father looked left and right and then, smiling a conspiratorial smile, whispered, "Yeah, for about ten seconds. And mind you, that was in third grade." He chuckled.

Jordan laughed. "What's said in here stays in here." He bumped fists with his father.

The bed squeaked as Mr. Mendoza rose to turn off the light. Jordan rolled one way, then the other, and soon drifted into sleep.

27

IN THE DREAM, Jordan approached Sierra, who stood, face lowered, looking at the puppy at her precious feet. Jordan said, "She's yours."

They were at the canal. The sky was ribbed with clouds all the way from Hawaii. The sun hung high over a cherry tree that yesterday had been bare but was now pink with blossoms. Jordan thought, *How is that possible?* It was November, not spring. Still, his being here with Sierra was also impossible. Love itself was impossible, especially when you had a bad, bad cold. And yet her presence seemed to heal him, to dry his sinuses like a big ole heat lamp.

"Please," Sierra encouraged him, "go ahead and play something."

Jordan brought out the harmonica. He tapped it against his palm, then blew one note—a honk. "I learned this from YouTube," he said, and began to play "Happy Birthday," his gaze locked on Sierra. He wanted to watch her every minute of the day.

"You're so good!" she sang.

"Thank you." He became bashful. "I'm working on

'Three Blind Mice,' but that's for another day. Right now," he continued, running one hand over the puppy's glossy fur, "she's yours."

Sierra dropped to her knees. "She's so cute."

"Dawn—that's her name."

"Dawn," Sierra mused, while the wind played in her most beautiful hair. "Like the dish soap?"

"No," said Jordan, "like the time of day when we wake up and our thoughts are filled with each other."

Jordan opened his eyes, startled and sweaty. He was feverish and frightened about something but wasn't sure what. He got out of bed, went to the kitchen, and drank a glass of water. He looked out the curtained window and thought about his dream. *Is this how people talk when they're in love?* Crazy stuff for sure. He closed his eyes. *Did I really play "Happy Birthday" on the harmonica?* He shook his head and decided that Dawn was a good name for a dog.

He retreated to bed, shivering from a cold draft, and scrolled his phone. There was a message from Coach and a few school announcements. But no message from either Sierra or Antonio.

"I'm alone," he muttered. And fell asleep.

Jordan sat up, pulling another Kleenex from the box on his bed. He looked at himself in the mirror. His eyes were half-closed, but the fraction that showed looked like red crayon scribblings on a white wall. "I have to go to school," he croaked.

"No you're not, Mr. Invalid," said his mom, carefully handing him a mug of chicken noodle soup.

"I gotta, Mom." Jordan sipped from the mug. "My life depends on it."

"Don't exaggerate. You're staying in bed even if I have to tie you down." Mrs. Mendoza was adamant. "If those policemen hadn't brought you in for questioning, you wouldn't be so sick."

"Mom, they were pretty nice. They just wanted to ask me some stuff."

"They could have asked you on the porch."

Jordan honked into a Kleenex and grimaced at the contents. He didn't know that such a green color existed in the spectrum.

"I should call the mayor," Mrs. Mendoza threatened.

"We have a mayor?"

"Yes, we have a mayor." She shook her head. "Your cold is affecting your brain."

Jordan's mother returned to the kitchen, but not before cracking open a window. "Fresh air. It'll be good for you." She sniffed the air. "Your bedroom smells. What's with boys?"

Jordan sipped the soup, smacking his lips at the rich

flavor. Maybe he would keep eating soup instead of cereal for breakfast even when he was all better. He reached for the harmonica on the nightstand, wet his lips, and tried to play "Three Blind Mice." The harmonica made noise but didn't offer a melody.

"She hates me," he moaned, tossing the harmonica aside. "And I don't blame her." He blinked back tears and ran a finger under his nose. He looked at his finger, then wiped it clean on a Kleenex. He reached for his phone: 7:48, no messages. He texted Antonio. "What's happening with you? I got a nose full of *mocos*." At 7:57, still nothing. But at 9:10 he got a text from Coach Ramirez, reminding him about after-school practice.

Jordan lowered his head on the pillow and moaned, "I'm in trouble." He fell asleep with his phone in his hand.

Jordan's dream featured some recurring elements. He and Sierra were standing on the bank of the canal. They were in love.

"So what am I in looks, from one to ten?" Jordan asked.

"With a flower in your hair, eleven," Sierra said, tucking a daisy behind one of his ears.

"And without?"

Sierra circled him, sizing him up. "A four," she concluded, then laughed, holding her hand over her mouth.

"Really? A four?"

Sierra shrugged and said brightly. "Afraid so!" She pressed herself against Jordan, then jumped into his arms. He staggered a few steps and then let his legs go weak. They tumbled to the sandy ground. "I'm glad I'm a four," he said. Then they kissed.

I'm ready to die of happiness, Jordan thought. *If only I had a cookie to accompany this feeling.*

They sat up.

"You mentioned a plastic bag," said Sierra, "the one that floated out of the car."

"What about it?" Jordan asked seriously.

"I think it floated downstream."

"Don't you think the cops would have searched for it?" Jordan asked, his tone resembling that of Detective Anderson, all police-y.

"Incompetence," Sierra suggested. "But let's not talk about them. Let's—"

Jordan startled awake. The phone in his hand had buzzed. He sat up and looked at a scolding text from Coach. "This is no time to be sick," he wrote. "Get your butt to practice this afternoon—and be on time!"

Jordan got out of bed and went to the bathroom. He washed his face and combed his hair, doing his best to look healthy. His mom was sitting in front of the computer in the den, pencil in hand.

"You're supposed to be in bed," she said.

"I'm thirsty." He drank a glass of water, then sat on a tall, swiveling stool. "Mom," he asked, "do you believe in dreams?"

"Nightmares yes, dreams no." She laughed, then went on. "Of course I believe in dreams. Why?"

"I don't know, just asking." Jordan eyed the clock: 10:13. *I should be in English*, he told himself, and then remembered the poem that Mrs. Roosevelt had recited. What was its title?

"I've gotta go to the bank," said his mom, sliding off her own stool.

"Pick me up some twenties," Jordan joked.

Jordan returned to his bedroom. Instead of getting back into bed, however, he got dressed. His mom believed in dreams, and he believed in them too, though they sometimes could be difficult to interpret.

He knew he should locate the plastic bag that had floated downstream. The police probably hadn't searched very far. Maybe it was snagged on a branch and bobbing near the bank. He needed to find out.

His mom shouted from the kitchen, "I'm going!"

"OK," he shouted back.

Jordan listened for the sounds of the front door opening and closing. He got up and ran to the living room, where he peeked out the front window. His mom was backing down the driveway, looking over her shoulder.

He rushed toward the back door, where the puppies were now caged behind a low, makeshift cardboard barrier. They barked their puppy barks as he stepped over the barrier, went outside, then put on his shoes. He rolled his bike out of the garage, thinking, *I have to ride fast.*

28

JORDAN LEANED OVER the bank of the canal and gazed downstream. Though it was late in the morning, the air was still cold, with frost whitening the ground. He was breathing hard from the ride and his breath hung like mist before his face, then broke apart. He blew his nose and readjusted his cap. His fingers were freezing—why hadn't he remembered to wear gloves? He pushed his hands into his pockets and shivered for a moment. Then he hid his bike in some bushes and started walking downstream.

He moved slowly, pushing through shrubs and clumps of ivy, climbing over fallen tree limbs and the occasional abandoned shopping cart. He half expected to encounter the homeless man who had given him the puppies, but knew it was unlikely.

Twenty minutes into his journey, he came upon a plastic bag bobbing like a pool toy in an eddy. Jordan scampered to the water's edge. With the help of a tree branch, he managed to prod it from the water. He carried it to a fallen log, sat down, and untied the knot. He hadn't known what to expect, but was still surprised by the bag's contents: several bundles of official-looking papers, along with two aluminum cookie boxes and an old windup alarm clock with the glass misted over. The clock had stopped at 8:47.

Jordan heard a twig snap somewhere in the brush. He looked around. An animal? A bird among the fallen leaves? The homeless man? Nervous, he threw the bag over his shoulder and started back toward his bike, tramping heavily through the wild undergrowth.

When he reached his bike, there was an older couple in the sandy area with their dog, an Irish setter. The dog looked up, wagging its tail slowly. Its mouth gripped a tennis ball.

"Hi," Jordan said. He rolled his bike over the cumbersome sand to the street. When he hopped aboard, the weight of the bag on his shoulder caused the bike to waver, but that didn't stop him. He rode away in a hurry, then paused, several blocks away, in the parking lot of a convenience store. He again inspected the contents of the bag: bundles of documents, the two aluminum boxes, and the old clock. Through the misted glass, he could see that the time now read 8:56. Had the clock come back to life?

He decided to open one of the boxes. He pried its lid off. Inside were ten stacks of fifty-dollar bills.

"Dang," Jordan muttered.

He picked up a stack and fanned the bills: the money smelled old. He replaced the stack and hammered the lid shut with his palm. The second box contained more stacks of fifty-dollar bills, along with a pocket watch attached to a long silver chain.

He nervously scanned the parking lot—no people, just a collection of trucks and beat-up cars. Then he gazed up at the sign on the convenience store. And found himself staring directly into the eye of a security camera.

Fear was a zipper running up and down his back. Jordan placed the cookie boxes back into the bag and glanced at the documents. They all seemed to carry the same name and address. *What should I do?* he asked himself. Take it to the police? No, he had a better idea.

He righted his bike and hopped back on, with the bag over his shoulder. He would take the bag's contents to the rightful owner himself—and do it before his mother returned home from the bank.

Ten minutes later, Jordan was straddling his bike and staring at a house with a scraggly lawn. His heart was beating wildly. Was it from the ride or from fear? There was a light on in what he imagined was the kitchen. He dismounted and set the bike quietly on the curb, then slowly approached the house, almost tiptoeing as he advanced up the driveway. He looked back: no one on the sidewalk, no one in their yard raking leaves, no one driving up the street. The neighbor's dog, however, was watching him intently, poised behind a chain-link fence.

"Don't bark," Jordan pleaded. He turned up the walkway and proceeded to the porch. He glanced in the window and saw an elderly woman seated at a table, her back to the world outside her house. He placed the plastic bag on the welcome mat, wheeled around, then leapt silently from the porch.

I did it! he thought, with pride. Then he glanced back, expecting the front door to open and the woman to appear. The door stayed closed, but what Jordan saw above the door frame sent a new rush of fear into his heart: another security camera.

Jordan was in bed, pajamas on, when his mother came into the bedroom.

"How do you feel?" she asked, sitting down on his bed. She put her hand on his forehead.

"Pretty good."

Jordan's mom pulled a leaf from his hair. She examined it closely, twirling the leaf by its stem. "Have you been somewhere?"

"Only in my dreams," Jordan lied, squeezing his eyes shut with remorse. Lying to your mom didn't seem like a good thing.

Mrs. Mendoza rose from the edge of the bed and opened the window a few more inches. She gazed at the side yard and remarked how the peach tree had lost its leaves. She turned and asked, "Would you like something to eat?"

Jordan asked for a burrito and a soda—root beer, if there was one available.

"In your dreams," his mom countered. "Sodas are bad for you."

After she left the room, Jordan checked his phone. He had a text from Antonio. "You're lucky to be in bed. I just fell asleep in algebra." It was almost one o'clock.

Jordan's mom returned with a mug of chicken noodle soup.

"Coach wants me at practice," Jordan announced brightly, trying to remove any hint of illness in his voice. His smiled, mouth closed.

"Oh, is that what he wants. Like, no. You're sick. You're not going anywhere."

"Mom, I'll be in trouble."

Mrs. Mendoza sat on the edge of the bed. "Did you take your last penicillin pill?"

"I did," Jordan said, showing her his hand, which no longer showed any trace of redness. "I feel great."

She looked doubtfully at him. "Jordan, you're sick. You want to end up in the hospital?"

"I'm not that sick, really."

At that very instant, Jordan felt an urge to blow his nose. But he willed himself not to bring a Kleenex to his face. He could feel the snot beginning to slide down. It was ready to drip from his nostrils when his mom finally relented.

"I'll drive you to practice," she said. "But you can't play. Just watch."

"Thanks, Mom. You're great."

"I know," she said, and got up from the edge of his bed.

It was hours before the start of practice. Jordan decided that he should rest. So he drank his soup and played a game called *Dragon Cage*. Then he searched YouTube for a harmonica lesson. The first lesson he found was for a song called "Red River Valley." He listened to this ancient cowboy song with a sour face, then mumbled, "People used to like this music?"

Finally he slept. When he woke, the room was dark. For a second he thought it was night, but then he saw that the curtains were closed, though moving slightly from a breeze that came through the open window.

Jordan blew his nose and dabbed a Kleenex at the corners of his watery eyes. "I can't," he admitted to himself. "I can't go to practice." His mom was right: he was sick.

Today was Monday and the championship game was on Wednesday. He texted Coach, then texted Ryan. "Man," he wrote, "I'm really, honestly, totally sick. Hope to be there tomorrow, really."

He waited to hear from them—nothing. Then he started to text Sierra, but stopped. He blew his nose, sank into his pillow, and slept again, with his phone off. No dreams visited him.

Two hours later, he woke to the sound of his father's truck pulling into the driveway. He coughed, stretched, and sat up. He felt a little better.

"Hey, honey," he heard his dad say in the kitchen. "How are the puppies?"

"Bunch of frisky troublemakers," said his mom. "Jordan is still sick."

Jordan turned on a lamp, its light casting a shadow across a poster of the Golden State Warriors. Mr. Mendoza entered the room and hovered by the bed.

"Mom says you're sick."

"Yeah, I am."

Jordan's dad sat on the edge of the bed. His face was the face of a tired plumber.

"I'm sick because I made myself sick."

"What does that mean?"

"It means that I lied to Mom," he blurted. He told his father about his dream, about the plastic bag and his desire to retrieve it.

Mr. Mendoza considered this information. Then he asked, "And was it there?"

Jordan nodded.

"Jordan," his dad sighed, "you can't do everything on your own."

"But I had the dream."

"Yeah, well, you don't have to act out *all* your dreams."

Jordan pondered his father's wisdom. "I returned the bag," he said.

"Returned it?"

Jordan described the bag's contents and explained how he had tiptoed up the woman's porch and left it.

Mr. Mendoza shook his head. "*No me digas.*" He cracked a knuckle. "So you went right to his house—"

"Her house."

"OK, her house." His forehead wrinkled as he thought about it. "Was she home?"

"Yeah, but I just left the bag. I saw her. She's an old woman."

"Correction—an elderly woman." He stared at Jordan. "Didn't you think that maybe you should have taken it to the police?"

Jordan lowered his face, suddenly worried. *Yeah,* he told himself. *I should have done that.* But how was he supposed to know? He was only thirteen. He looked up at his dad. "I guess so."

"You guess so," his father repeated. He let those words hang in the air before he roared, "Of course you should have! Or brought it home so that *I* could have taken it to the police." He growled under his breath.

"Did I do bad?" Jordan asked.

"Yeah, well . . . you didn't know. I mean, you were trying to do good. That's what counts." His dad got up from the bed and absently went to the chest of drawers. He picked up a third-place trophy, dusted it with his sleeve, then put it back down. He faced Jordan again. "When's your game?"

"Wednesday."

"Are you going to practice?"

Jordan shrugged.

"It's better you rest."

Jordan nodded. "Dad?" he asked, not wanting the conversation to end. "You know what you said about security cameras everywhere?"

"Not really, but they *are* everywhere. Why?"

"Because this woman—this house—had a security camera."

Jordan's father bit his lower lip and reseated himself on the bed's edge. "You think that camera caught you?"

Jordan nodded.

"But you know—and I know—that you didn't do anything wrong. You just returned what you found. You were being a Good Samaritan."

"I know, Dad, but it's—"

At that moment the front doorbell chimed: a musical *ding-dong*. Jordan and his father looked at each other. While Mr. Mendoza went to the door, Jordan got out of bed and put on his clothes. They were about to have some company.

29

JORDAN AGAIN SAT in the small, window-less room. He was dressed in jeans, a hoodie, his winter coat, and a cap. In his closed fist, he gripped a large ball of Kleenex.

Detective Anderson sauntered into the room, followed a few seconds later by Detective Jefferson.

Detective Jefferson snapped his fingers and pointed at Jordan. "Say, you're not the boy who was here yesterday, are you?"

Jordan squeezed his Kleenex. Then he covered his mouth and coughed.

The two detectives sat down in front of Jordan.

"Still got a cold?" Detective Jefferson asked.

Jordan nodded.

Detective Jefferson turned to Detective Anderson. "Maybe this boy isn't taking his vitamins."

"Is that true?" Detective Anderson asked. "No vitamin C in your system?"

Jordan didn't answer. The three sat quietly for nearly a minute before Detective Anderson tapped the folder on the table with a pencil. "You know why you're here, don't you?"

Jordan nodded yes.

"Then tell us why."

Jordan hesitated, then replied, "You see, I had this dream."

Both detectives immediately doubled over in laughter.

"Not another dream," Detective Jefferson said. He raked a tear from the corner of his eye. "First it was the puppy—"

"Puppies," Jordan corrected him.

"Then the dream about the girl, then a dream about more dogs, and now a dream about all this cash?" Detective Jefferson wagged his head. "Son, you got me laughing."

"Does it matter if it was a short dream?"

"Short dream?" Detective Anderson fumed. "I don't care if it was short, long, in color, in black and white, or in a foreign language. What's with you, son?"

Jordan blew his nose, twice. He had an answer for this question and he supplied it. "I'm thirteen."

The detectives turned to one another, smirking. What sort of response was that?

Detective Anderson began to tap his pencil against the folder. "You were caught on surveillance video in front of a convenience store and then at Mrs. Rodriguez's house. How did you get that bag?"

"Like I told you," he began, and recounted his earlier story of swimming out to see if someone had been trapped in the Honda. When he'd opened the passenger-side door, a black plastic bag had floated out and away downstream.

"Then you had this last dream and went looking for it?" asked Detective Anderson.

"Yeah," cried a hopeful Jordan. "It was, like, maybe a half mile down the canal."

"A half mile from where we found the Honda in the water?"

Jordan nodded. "If you had looked, you would have found it."

"You telling us how to do our job?" Detective Jefferson asked, knitting his eyebrows.

Jordan remained quiet. He could hear the ticking of their wristwatches. He wished for nothing more than to be in bed playing *Dragon Cage*—or at basketball practice, feeling healthy and going up for one layup after another.

"I know you don't believe me," Jordan said, finally breaking the silence.

More stares from the detectives. Then Detective Anderson asked, "Do you consider yourself a liar and a thief?"

"Nah, Anderson," interrupted Detective Jefferson. "This boy is a dreamer."

"I don't steal and I don't lie," Jordan protested. He

knew that he'd lied to his mom about leaving the house, but that didn't count here, he figured. "I keep my promises, always."

The two detectives looked at each other. They were on the verge of laughter.

"What we have here," Detective Jefferson began, "is a Boy Scout, true to his word." His smile grew thin. "Tell me, Jordan, what promise have you kept recently?"

"It's something private," Jordan replied. "I can't say."

"Can't or won't?" asked Detective Anderson.

"Is there a difference?" inquired Jordan.

The two detectives looked at each other again. They laughed this time, but their laughter was soon replaced with scowls.

"Jordan, do you know where you are and why?" Detective Jefferson asked, his eyes narrowing.

Jordan raised his eyes to the ceiling and wondered what was on the second floor of the building. For a second, he imagined boys sitting on dirty mattresses in their cells.

"We're talking to you!" barked Detective Anderson.

Jordan startled but didn't say anything.

"Let me answer that for you," Detective Jefferson said calmly. "You are at juvie. You are suspected of robbery, and of transporting drugs. And we found a gun in the Honda."

Detective Anderson spoke up. "But Detective, this boy is not a criminal. No, this is a boy who doesn't lie and always keeps his promises."

"Yeah," said Detective Jefferson, gazing at Jordan. "Son, let me ask again. What promise did you make recently?"

Jordan swallowed. "If I tell you," he said, "you won't tell anyone else?"

"Whatever you say stays among us," Detective Anderson replied, gesturing with his large hands at the three of them. "Stays right here in this room. How's that, Jordan?"

"OK," said Jordan, deciding to open up. "I told my friend . . ."

"What friend?" Detective Anderson asked.

"A friend from school."

"What's his name?" they both chimed in.

"Antonio. The one with the piccolo. I promised that I wouldn't tell anyone that he plays it. But then," Jordan continued, "Antonio said it was OK if I told others about it. See, he's in the pep band and he's going to be playing at the game, so people are going to know anyhow. Know what I mean?" Jordan paused, looking from one detective to the other. "But I kept my promise until he said it was OK."

The two detectives stared at Jordan.

"Pep band," Detective Jefferson mused. "Let me guess. That girl you like?"

"Sierra," Jordan said.

"She's in the band too," Detective Jefferson continued. "Correct?"

"Correct."

"Did you by chance make her any promises?"

"I did."

"And?"

"I can't say."

"Can't say?" Detective Anderson said. "You know where you are again?"

"Juvie."

"And at juvie we search for the truth. So, what did you promise her?"

"I told her—in my heart, I mean—that I would love her forever."

The two detectives blinked at Jordan, then blinked at each other. This boy was a real comedian!

Jordan was back in bed, finishing his third helping of chicken noodle soup for the day. And he was still hungry. He hadn't expected that a police interrogation would famish him. His stomach rumbled as he lifted the spoon to his mouth.

"I told them the truth, Mom," he said.

"But you didn't tell *me* the truth," she replied. "You said that you hadn't left the house." She feigned hurt feelings, but she was not a good actor. Her eyes shone and Jordan could tell that she was glad her son was home, in bed, with noodles slithering down his throat.

Jordan lowered his gaze. He was on the mend, but he still didn't feel good about lying to his mother. "I know. And I'm sorry."

Mrs. Mendoza sighed. She picked up Jordan's phone, which lay on the bed. Its face glowed 9:36. "Do you think you can go to school tomorrow?"

"I'd rather stay home. But could I go to practice?"

Jordan's mom released another sigh. "Are you good?"

Jordan was uncertain by what she meant by "good"—a good son, maybe?

"At basketball," said his mother.

"GOOD?" Jordan sat up, with his game face on. "Mom, you know what the word *star* means?"

"You mean like in the night sky?" She pointed a mani- cured finger toward the ceiling.

"No, I mean a player who scores and scores, a player who lives for the roar of the crowd!"

Mrs. Mendoza felt his cheek for a fever. "You should stay home," she said. "I think you're delirious again."

At that, she left Jordan's bedroom and went to check on the barking puppies.

30

JORDAN STAYED HOME again on Tuesday morning, playing video games and listening to music. But after three hours, he was bored. He moved from his bed to the couch, then back to bed. The puppies followed him, their ears flopping, their tails wagging. He felt for the littlest one, Dawn. She had barely survived, and now was loved.

"Dawn," he said, holding her against his chest, "you're special." When he gave her a gentle squeeze, she squeaked like a toy.

Jordan was drinking a cup of hot chocolate, a single marshmallow floating on top, when Antonio called.

"What, you ain't coming to school again?"

"I'm sick, sort of. And *ain't* isn't a proper word."

"It ain't?"

During their discussion of the nutritional value of nachos for breakfast, a text from Sierra arrived, asking if she could call him during morning break. It was 10:35. The break was now!

"I gotta go," Jordan told Antonio, cutting him off.

"No, bro, I gotta go," said Antonio. He hung up first.

Jordan texted Sierra back, "Yes, call." Dabbing his nose with a Kleenex, he watched the screen. When the call came, he let the phone ring three times before answering.

"Jordan," Sierra began without hesitation. "I'm moving away."

Jordan swallowed in disbelief. *Did he hear right?* "What did you say?" he asked.

"My mom got a job transfer. We're moving to some place called Glendale." She hesitated before stating the obvious: "I know you like me."

Jordan swallowed again. "Sierra, it's more than *like*." He shot a glance at his bedroom door when he heard his mom's footsteps going from the living room to the kitchen. He turned back to his phone. "I mean," he said desperately, "I'm ready to give you a dog. So it's more than like."

"One of the puppies, you mean?"

"Yeah, that's what I mean. I'm really sorry that your dog died."

"Thank you, Jordan. She was a good dog—a great dog, really."

There was silence on both ends of the connection. Jordan could hear his heart thumping beneath the wheezing in his lungs. Then, through the phone, he heard the school bell ringing.

"I have to go," Sierra said.

"Don't go," Jordan begged.

"I have to, Jordan."

After Sierra hung up, Jordan studied her image on his phone. He regretted not using the word *love*. That's what he felt and that's what it was—love. The detectives could laugh all they wanted!

He heard scratching at the bedroom door and got out of bed. When he cracked it open, in pranced Dawn. The puppy looked up at Jordan. There was happiness in her eyes, happiness in her body. She began to sniff around the room, tail wagging.

"Get over here," called Jordan, returning to the bed.

Dawn approached, nostrils sniffing the air. When Jordan lifted her up, she gave a slight groan. She was so innocent, Jordan thought, so new to this world. He hugged her, though not as hard as his pillow, and whispered in her floppy ear, "You're going to live with a beautiful girl."

Jordan talked his mom into driving him to school. He was feeling better, he told her, and he was—all that sleep had really helped. He was eager to talk to Sierra, but the first person he saw was Antonio, walking up the steps to Main Hall.

"Hey, dude," Antonio said. "You better?"

"Yeah, a little better."

"You know what?"

"What?"

"I'm gonna make the piccolo something cool."

Man, here he goes, Jordan thought.

"Like, yeah. I mean, I'm gonna introduce the piccolo to rap, make it the go-to instrument, blow everything up in a big way. You feel me?"

"Rap? As in rap music?"

"Yeah, I'm gonna be a pioneer, like Lizzo and the flute." Antonio said that he had just written a rap called "East Side Piccolo." He admitted that he was breaking new ground, but he was determined to succeed. "I tell you—"

"Have you seen Sierra?"

"Man, you like interrupted me."

"Sorry, but I need to know. Have you seen her?"

Antonio stroked his chin, pondering the question. He snapped his fingers and said, "Yeah, I saw her holding hands with a fifth grader who, like, infiltrated our school."

"Tony, that ain't even funny."

"WHAT! First, *ain't* ain't a proper word. Second, it *was* funny. Third, these days I go by Antonio—remember?" He scanned their surroundings. "Honestly, I haven't seen her. But we have band practice right after school."

Jordan had basketball practice after school—a conflict. To change the subject, he confided, "I was in juvie last night."

"WHAT!"

"And the day before."

"WHAT!

"I was interrogated by the police."

"Like, dang, I could use that experience. Get me some rhymes for my piccolo piece. So what happened?"

"I'll explain later," Jordan said. He had caught sight of Sierra walking with Ashley. They were smiling and talking. But when her eyes met his, hers became a dark cloud.

"Sierra!" he called.

Sierra stopped and Ashley peeled away.

"I can't talk right now." She gazed down the hallway full of students. "I have class."

"I have class too."

"Really," she said, "I can't talk right now." Then she wheeled around and, with a skip, pushed off down the hall.

Why? Jordan wondered. *Why couldn't you talk?* He went to his US history class. No one seemed to have missed him, except Ryan Greene. The two bumped fists.

"Heard you were hecka sick. What's with that?"

Jordan sat down at his desk and fired up his laptop. The word *sick*, he thought, could be taken in many different ways. But *lovesick*, he felt, described him best. He sniffled and said, "Just a cold."

"But you're ready to play, ain't you?"

With Pedro out, the team needed all its players. Jordan didn't know how much he would be able to contribute on the court. His lungs continued to rattle whenever he took a deep breath. Still, he was committed.

"I'm ready," he said, rolling a hand into a fist. "For sure we're gonna beat 'em." Jordan couldn't be certain why he had made this promise, but it seemed like the right thing to say.

They bumped fists again and class began.

When school was over for the day, Jordan spotted Sierra among the hordes of departing students. She was making her way to the cafeteria for band practice. He was about to call out to her when Ryan put an arm on his shoulder.

"Let's do it," he said.

Jordan had no choice but to follow Ryan to the gym.

When they were suited up in their jerseys, Coach asked, "You feeling better? I was worried about you."

"Yeah," Jordan said, "way better."

They began with drills by running up and down the court, then switched to sidesteps. To hone their defensive skills, they backpedaled with their arms held out to the sides.

"Keep it up!" Coach yelled. "They can't get by you if your arms are out."

Jordan's lungs burned from exhaustion. Still, he kept his arms out and kept his feet moving. During the drill, he had noticed that he no longer felt sick. He was just breathing hard.

The team practiced layups, rebounding, setting screens, shooting free throws.

"Guys lookin' good!" Coach roared, clapping his hands. "Now for a friendly," he said, sorting the boys into two teams.

This time, Jordan found himself on the B team. Was this because he had missed Monday practice, he wondered, or had someone else proved himself better? His replacement was Simon.

Really? Jordan debated with himself. *Simon is better?*

The A team beat the B team in a ten-minute game, 18–9. Jordan managed two baskets—a layup and a mid-range shot. Simon also scored two baskets. Did this mean that they were equally good, or equally average? Jordan had missed two shots and had a hard time keeping up with the player he was guarding. He was out of shape, he realized. Plus, he still had a cold, even though he felt better.

After showering, Jordan walked home, with the burden of a backpack on his shoulder and the uncertainty of his life inside his head. He texted Sierra, "When are you moving?" He wondered if she was really moving. Had he heard her right? Maybe she was just transferring to a new school. Sierra didn't text back.

The three puppies greeted him at the back door by attacking his pant cuffs. He unlatched their teeth from the fabric and hugged each one. "What do you think you are? Guard dogs?" He brought all three into his arms and went into the house, kicking his shoes off at the back door. "I've been to juvie. Guess you guys know a bad boy when you see one."

Jordan's mother appeared in the kitchen. "How do you feel?" she asked.

"OK," he answered. Inhaling, Jordan noticed only a faint wheeze in his chest.

His mom rattled a bottle of vitamin C. "Here," she said. "I should have started you on them earlier."

Jordan uncapped the bottle and shook two tablets into his palm. He chewed them down, then announced, "Sierra's moving away."

"I know," Mrs. Mendoza replied.

"You know?"

"TikTok."

Of course. Jordan had been avoiding TikTok because of the posts that mocked his missed layup. They were everywhere, it seemed. Along with an image of him in the air with his tongue out.

His mom ran a warm hand up and down Jordan's arm. "We're still going to give her the littlest one," she said affectionately. "Is that OK?"

Jordan felt sad, but he agreed—Dawn would go with Sierra.

"Good," his mom said, then glanced at his bedroom. "You have a guest, by the way."

Jordan was bewildered. *A guest?*

When he opened the bedroom door, Antonio was there, listening to music. He pulled off his earbuds.

"Hey, check out my ride!" he hollered. He pounded the handlebars, threw a leg over the bar, and dismounted. "A thousand dollars."

"That much?"

"OK, seven hundred dollars."

"Seven hundred?"

"OK, three hundred and twenty-seven dollars. It's used." He lifted the bike with his pinkie finger. "Look," he crowed. "It's super light." He leaned it against the wall.

"How used?"

Antonio stroked his chin familiarly. "I think I'm the fourth owner, not counting the time it got stole. But I'm not here about the bike."

"Bet you want to eat dinner with us."

"Nah, dude. I'm here to do something special for you." With that, he pulled a sharp felt-tip pen from his pocket. To Jordan, it looked like a large hypodermic needle. "I'm here to ink you up."

Jordan jumped back. "Ink me up? Are you crazy? He eyeballed the pen. "I don't want to bleed."

"Nah, dude, it won't break your skin." Antonio recounted their venture into the creepy tattoo shop. He said that Jordan was too young for the real thing, but on the eve of the big game he needed every advantage he could get. A tattoo might give him confidence and help him play like the pros. The ink would come off in the shower, Antonio promised. "So what's it going to be?"

"Antonio, you're crazy."

"Not crazy—creative!" Antonio rolled up his sleeve, revealing the words "Piccolo Rapper" inked onto his forearm.

Jordan's jaw dropped open. He peered more closely at Antonio's work. He had to admit that the penmanship was superb, even cool. He let go of Antonio's arm and said, "No way."

"OK, be that way, but you know . . ." Antonio hesitated. "I'm here to complete your destiny."

"My destiny?"

"I'm here to add to your brown skin the most beautiful name in the entire universe: Sierra." He smiled. "You ever hear such a beautiful name? Besides mine, of course."

So Jordan allowed Antonio to write "Sierra" on his right bicep, laughing throughout the experience because he was so ticklish. In the end, the temporary tattoo was artfully done. Every time Jordan flexed his bicep, Sierra's name grew larger.

Yeah, Jordan reflected. *Maybe a tattoo will make me play better.* After all, most pro basketball players were seriously inked up.

31

"**ANTONIO'S BIKE** looks expensive," Mr. Mendoza said, looking from Jordan to his wife and then back to Jordan. "Where did he steal it?"

"Dad!" scolded Jordan.

Jordan's father lifted his napkin up to his mouth and began to chuckle.

Mrs. Mendoza slapped her husband's forearm. "You're awful," she said. "Antonio wouldn't steal. You know that."

"That's right," Jordan's dad said. "He plays the piccolo. Musicians only steal other people's songs." His chuckle became laughter.

"That's enough out of you," Jordan's mom warned. She faked a frown.

"It's really light," Jordan said. "A present from his mom." He looked down at his phone and started scrolling.

Mr. Mendoza reached over and took Jordan's phone away. "All thoughts on your mom's cooking," he said, placing it in his shirt pocket.

When Jordan's phone started to ring, he didn't dare ask for it back. He had to agree with his dad—his mom was a good cook. He gave her a thumbs-up sign and said, "You make the best grub, Mom."

"Why, thank you, my sick son."

"Phones have no place at the dinner table," said Jordan's father, reaching for a tortilla. He turned to his wife. "How did we communicate when we were young?"

"By screaming," she replied, laughing and stroking Jordan's hair. "He's feeling better."

"I can tell," Jordan's dad agreed. "Look, he's licked his plate and is getting up for thirds."

"Seconds, Dad," Jordan corrected him as he headed toward the stove. His phone rang again, and again he didn't dare ask for it back.

"When's the game?" his father asked, after Jordan returned to the table.

"Ay, *viejo*, you know," said Jordan's mom. "I told you a dozen times."

Mr. Mendoza offered his wife a playful smirk. He had written it down and posted it on the refrigerator: Tomorrow, Wednesday, 4:15. He was living for that game, along with a second helping of chili verde.

"I'll be there straight from work."

Jordan reached for the basket of tortillas. "I'm not starting. Coach probably won't put me in until late in the game."

"*¿Por qué no?*"

"Because I missed practice. Simon is going to start."

"Simon? Who's Simon?"

"Another seventh grader on the team. He's pretty good."

The family continued eating in silence. Jordan's father finished his second helping, then pushed away his plate. He balled up his paper napkin and tossed it onto the plate. "*Amor,*" he nodded to his wife, "*muy rico.*"

"Glad you liked it," she replied, rising to her feet. "Because you're having it tomorrow—and the next day." She squinted at her husband's plate. "Now I know our son takes after his father—your plate is licked clean too." She inspected the fork. "And the fork—it could go back in the drawer."

Mr. Mendoza smiled, then turned his attention to Jordan. "Tomorrow, the final game. You going to kick their butts?"

"Yeah, it's the championship."

"Should we build a trophy shelf?"

"Dad, don't. You might jinx us. Can I have my phone back?"

"In a bit," said his mother. "Let your food digest. The world will wait."

Jordan remained quiet even when the phone began to ring a third time. Mr. Mendoza pulled the phone out of his pocket and looked at it, wagged his head, and said in a low, playful whisper, "The piccolo player." He put the phone back into his shirt pocket and tapped the tabletop with his palm. "Hey, I hear our littlest puppy has a home."

The idea of parting with Dawn—and Sierra—truly pained Jordan. He envisioned himself handing over the puppy, then teary-eyed Sierra getting into a car and driving away. At first, he imagined that she would look back. But then he revised the scene. No, he thought, she and the puppy would drive off without a backward glance. And he, Jordan Mendoza, would no longer be a part of Sierra's life or the puppy's life.

"Where are we?" asked Jordan's dad, waving a hand in front of his face. "Are you still with us?"

"Sorry," Jordan said. "I was just thinking."

Mr. Mendoza rose from his chair. "I'm gonna watch some television. Here's your phone."

Jordan went straight to TikTok. There was a new posting from Antonio. It showed a bowl of menudo with the caption, "A snack before dinner."

Next he opened a text from Sierra that read, "Hope you're feeling better."

He texted back. "Lots better."

Jordan took a few steps toward his bedroom, then turned back to the kitchen. His mother was loading the dirty dishes into the dishwasher. He told her that dinner was great, then hugged her and pointed to his phone. "It's Sierra," he said. "I gotta talk to her."

His mom smiled but didn't say anything.

Jordan closed the door to his bedroom and, heart thumping, made the call. She picked up on the first ring.

"It's me," Jordan said.

"I know."

Silence.

"When are you moving?"

"This weekend, maybe Friday."

He had been sitting on the edge of his bed but sprang to his feet. "So soon?"

"Yeah."

Jordan couldn't help himself. "I'm going to miss you," he said.

"I'm going to miss you too."

He sat back down, a sudden pain in his heart. He closed his eyes and imagined Sierra in the car driving away. She was in the back seat, peering through the window, waving goodbye after all. She held up one of Dawn's paws, so the puppy could wave goodbye too.

"Your mom can't find a job here?"

"My mom works for a bank. She has to go where they tell her."

"Really?"

"She got promoted."

"What's promoted?"

"It's like when you get a better job, more money. That's the way it is."

Jordan swallowed. "And your dad?"

"My parents are divorced. I thought you knew that."

Jordan grimaced. *So thoughtless*, he told himself. *You did know that.*

Again Sierra asked, "Are you feeling better?"

Jordan took a deep breath. "Pretty good," he said.

"So are you playing tomorrow?"

Jordan didn't want to talk about basketball. He wanted to talk about her, about them, about how he was feeling. "I had a dream about you," he confessed.

Silence.

"We were at the canal and I asked you a question."

"What did you ask me?" Sierra replied, after a moment's hesitation.

"I know it sounds stupid," he said, but he told her anyway. In the dream, he had asked her to rate his looks on a scale from one to ten. "You told me I was a four."

Sierra laughed. "That good?" she asked playfully.

Jordan nearly screamed with happiness. "That's exactly what you said in my dream!" He took another deep breath. "But then you changed your mind. You said I was, like, a ten—or I think you did. It was a dream, you know."

"That's a nice dream."

Jordan was silent for several seconds. "Will you really miss me?" he asked, grimacing at his tone. *Was this too pathetic?*

"Of course," said Sierra, then announced, "Jordan, I can't accept the puppy."

"You can't? Why?"

"I know that your mom—she's great—promised me the puppy. But," she explained, "our new apartment doesn't allow dogs."

The scene inside Jordan's head changed. Sierra was still in the back seat, waving goodbye. But without the pup, he knew for certain that she would forget him.

"I have to go," Sierra said. "My mom wants me to help her. We're packing things, cleaning the kitchen, stuff like that." She wouldn't be at school tomorrow, she added, but she would be at the game.

"The pep band, of course," Jordan mumbled.

But neither hung up immediately. Somehow, the silence between them was almost comforting. Jordan moved his phone from one ear to the other. Finally, he asked, "Does that mean we can't see each other, like in the future?"

"No, it doesn't mean that. Not at all." She told him to rest up for the game. Then: "I should go."

After Sierra hung up, Jordan lay back on his bed. He felt something worse than sadness. Sierra was moving away. He grabbed his harmonica and began to play "Red River

Valley." Only then, in the near dark of his bedroom, could he understand why others—in another place and another era—might have appreciated the song. It was about pain.

That night he did his homework—algebra, history, civics, and, lastly, language arts, his favorite class. Although the assignment was to read a few chapters of a novel, he found himself thinking of the poem that Mrs. Roosevelt had read aloud.

Jordan got a text from Coach. "You won't start but you'll get your minutes. Meet at the gym no later than 3:15. Be on time, we're the traveling team." They would be bused to the school where the game would be held.

He checked Antonio's TikTok. It showed a photo of him wearing a paper napkin like a bib tucked into his collar. He was chowing down on a huge bowl of fried rice.

Food, Jordan mused. *That's all the dude thinks about.* He took off his T-shirt and examined his tattoo. He flexed his bicep and ran a finger over the small bulb of muscle. He laughed at himself. Love, he had discovered, could be both fun and sad.

He finished his homework, dressed in his pajamas, then went into the living room.

"I'm going to bed," he announced.

Mr. Mendoza, sunk comfortably in his recliner, glanced up and muted the television. "Heard you playing

'Red River Valley,'" he said.

Jordan was surprised. "You know that song?"

"I do." His dad smiled and placed his hands on his stomach. "There was a movie by that name. An old Western. Good film."

Jordan kissed his mom good night. He paused, then told her that Sierra wouldn't be taking the puppy.

"She's not?" Her face showed worry.

"She and her mom are moving into an apartment that doesn't allow dogs."

"Oh," his mom replied. She kissed Jordan and she pushed him off gently in the direction of his bedroom.

Jordan lay in bed and looked at Sierra's image on his phone while the melody of "Red River Valley" played over and over in his thoughts. After a while, he switched off the phone and sank into a dark void of sleep.

32

JORDAN WOKE at the sound of the back door closing—his father was off to work. He got up, went to the bathroom, and looked at himself in the mirror. He went through a set of expressions: smile, grimace, scowl, laugh, then smile again. *Two days ago*, he thought, *I had a really bad cold*. He still had some sniffles this morning, but he was feeling much better.

He stripped off his pajama top and examined the tattoo, which was beginning to smear. When he flexed his bicep, the name seemed to explode in size. He laughed at himself, then returned to his bedroom to get dressed for the day.

He ate breakfast—two bowls of cereal—then was off to school. On the drive, his mom lip-synched to a 90s song on the car radio. He hoped none of his classmates would see. A block from campus, she pulled to the curb.

"Do you have all your gym stuff?"

He peered into his bag: team jersey, team sweatshirt, an extra T-shirt, extra pair of briefs, shoes, mouth guard (which he never used), athletic supporter, water bottle, protein bar, and two pairs of socks with blue and red stripes, the colors of their school.

"I'm good," he said, then allowed his mom to kiss him on the cheek.

In his morning classes, Jordan only half listened to his teachers. He couldn't get Sierra out of his thoughts. At lunch with Antonio, he ate a single slice of cheese pizza and a bag of potato chips. They sat together in the quad, at a table far from the milling students. The mood between them was somber.

"She's leaving," Jordan remarked after his pizza was gone.

"Sorry, bro." To honor his friend's feelings, Antonio stopped eating his second slice. "I kinda knew that."

"You did?"

"Yeah, you know, Ashley said something." Antonio shook his head. "Sad, really. Where's she going?"

"Some place called Glendale."

"You could still be, like, friends."

"Just friends?"

"Yeah, friends are good. That's what I think."

Jordan shrugged and had to wonder—*Can a girl you love just be a friend?* He looked at his potato chips and waited for an answer, but nothing came.

When the school bell rang, they rose to their feet and returned to class.

During the second break in the afternoon, Jordan decided to spend his time alone. He cruised the baseball field where two sixth graders he had seen wrestling each other were now sharing a soda. They were friends after all.

In the distance, he could make out four adults walking toward him. They grew larger and larger, like ships appearing through a fog.

"Jordan!" one of them called.

It was Mr. Hollister, the vice principal, another man he didn't recognize, plus Detectives Anderson and Jefferson, both of whom were smiling. *Smiling at me?* Jordan wondered. *What had he done now?*

"Jordan, my boy," Mr. Hollister said, patting his shoulder. He turned to the detectives and crowed, "He's one of our finest athletes."

Finest athletes?

"Great academics!"

You mean my Cs in algebra, history, and social studies?

Jordan had seen his share of crime-fighting TV shows. He was aware that, once caught, any sensible criminal would put his hands behind his back and get ready for the cuffs. Through the huddle of adults that surrounded him, he could see some students approaching. Something different was happening on campus, and they would be curious. All of them were eating potato chips or candy.

"Do I have to go back to juvie?" Jordan asked.

"We're not arresting you, Jordan," said Detective Anderson. "Why would we think of that?"

Detective Jefferson stood grinning with his mouth closed. The person next to him—a guy with long hair and two cameras on his shoulder—was also grinning.

"Nah," Detective Anderson went on. "You're a solid citizen. Truthfully, I wish there were more like you."

Solid citizen?

"That's right," agreed Detective Jefferson. "We're here to congratulate you." He was grinning so hard now that his teeth showed.

"What did I do?" Jordan asked aloud.

"You returned Mrs. Rodriguez's hard-earned money, that's what."

"She was so touched," Detective Anderson explained.

Jordan pictured the black plastic bag sitting on the welcome mat at the elderly woman's house.

"You rescued her life's savings, along with some important legal documents."

The man with the cameras introduced himself as a photographer from the local newspaper. He positioned

Jordan between the detectives and snapped three quick photos.

"One of our finest athletes," Mr. Hollister exclaimed again. "Stellar student, nice parents, puppies at home—the works!" He ruffled Jordan's hair. "Next year, he'll run for vice president of his class."

"Vice president?" Jordan mumbled.

"Maybe president. Who knows? But remember, you'll be up against Jazmin Cortez—she's no joke."

This, Jordan thought, *is very, very weird*. A few minutes ago, he'd been ready to weep over Sierra's imminent departure from his life. Now this? Praise from the vice principal and two detectives, with a photographer snapping his picture every few seconds? *Yeah*, he concluded. *A very, very weird moment*.

The photographer spoke up. "I hear you're playing in a basketball championship."

"Yeah, us against the Bears."

"We Patriots," Vice Principal Hollister began. "We have a strong tradition in sports. It's because of boys like Jordan." He patted Jordan's shoulder again.

"I'll be at the game," the photographer announced, holding up his camera.

"Wish we could be there too," Detective Jefferson remarked. "But we've got crime to fight. Some troublemaker out there could be putting his handprints in wet cement."

"Before we leave," Detective Anderson said, "we have something for you." He produced an envelope from his breast pocket. "Mrs. Rodriguez wrote you a thank-you letter."

When the adults walked away, the student onlookers quickly lost interest. In their place a few pigeons landed and began to peck at the spilled potato chips.

Jordan opened the letter. It read: *Thank you for saving my money. You are a good, good boy. Here's a little something for you. I hope you go to college.*

Jordan plucked a fifty-dollar bill from the envelope. The money felt stiff between his fingers, as if it had dried after getting damp, riding the waves of a dirty canal.

33

NOW THAT THE DETECTIVES and reporter had gone, Sierra elbowed her way back into Jordan's mind. He stared longingly at her image on his phone. He texted her: "See you soon." He considered adding, "You're the most beautiful girl since Juliet," but worried that might scare her. Plus, he couldn't really compare himself to Romeo. *No*, he thought, *I'm more like Justin Bieber—without the tattoos.*

Instead, he typed: "I look forward to hearing you on the glockenspiel. I heard how it sounds on YouTube. It's awesome."

Sierra texted back within minutes. "No, you're awesome." At that, Jordan almost started to cry. First his parents called him a hero, then the vice principal called him a fine athlete, and now a girl called him awesome. *Was any of this true?*

At 3:00 he was sitting on the bus. One after another the team members piled in, cheering wildly. They were devouring candy bars, chewing on Red Whips, and shaking bags of potato chips down their throats. They were shoving each other, yelling and cursing in both English and Spanish. Some were hitting each other with their gym bags. Others were recording the mayhem on their phones. But this pregame ritual halted when Coach boarded, followed by his assistant, a college student named Bradley who was as tall as a giraffe.

Coach scanned the commotion with fire in his eyes. He reached over and pulled a Red Whip dangling from one player's mouth. "No candy!" he ordered.

The assistant coach counted the team members, then shouted, "Are you ready?"

The entire team yelled, "Yeah!"

"Who are WE?" Coach yelled in reply.

"The Patriots!"

"Now sit down and don't goof around—focus. You got a mission!"

Coach and his assistant sat in the front seats, arms crossed over their chests as if they would accept nothing but victory.

As the bus pulled away from the gym, its tailpipe belching black puffs of smoke, Jordan gazed out the window. It was a fresh view for him. He seldom rode up so high, and the change in perspective made him view his school in a different light. It was its own world, with its own rules and even its own history. How many times in the past had busloads of student athletes ridden down this same driveway, over the same potholes? On the way to victory, on the way to defeat, on the way to something like a battle. The bus, elephant slow, approached the school exit, swaying gently. A crowd of students waved from the parking lot. Jordan waved back. He heard someone shout, "Go get 'em. Kick their butts!"

Jordan knew that he wouldn't be starting the game. Still, when called upon, he would do his best. He made a mental list of what to do on the court. *Feed the ball to Ryan*, he told himself. *Don't take any foolish shots. Defend. Keep your arms out. Above all, don't foul and give the opponent a free throw.*

As the bus bumped along, the players quieted. Jordan imagined that most of them were making their own mental lists. Ryan, however, was playing a game on his phone. He was relaxed and confident. Simon, sitting next to Ryan, had his earbuds on. His knee was jerking to the music.

The bus rolled onto the freeway; two exits later, it turned off the freeway and moved down a commercial street. At a red light, Jordan caught sight of a man with his hand thrust into a city garbage can chained to a bus stop bench. His unwashed hair shot out at angles from his head and his skin was gray as ash. When he looked up, his eyes met Jordan's.

"Dang," Jordan muttered. It was the same homeless

man from the canal. He was saying something, mouthing the words. Then he raised a hand that could have signaled either *hello* or *goodbye*.

The bus jerked into motion again. Jordan sat back, eyes closed, and remembered the man handing him the fourth pup, now named Dawn. It had been the nicest gift ever.

A half hour later, the team disembarked in orderly fashion. They were quiet as they headed to the locker room. The gymnasium was very modern, nothing like their old place. Jordan could sense the anxiety, even fear, among his teammates. They were in unfamiliar territory. The Bears were really good. They had gone undefeated during league play, while they, the Patriots, had been 5–2.

In the locker room, the players stripped off their street clothes and wrestled themselves into their jerseys. They laced up their shoes, then stretched. Some players moved crablike, sidling left and right. Others jumped in place, bringing their knees to their chests.

Jordan examined the tattoo on his arm. He could still make out Sierra's name, but it was getting blurrier. He kissed his bicep and laughed to himself.

"This is it!" Coach yelled, slamming his palm against a locker. "Who are we?"

"The Patriots!" the team roared.

"That's right, that's who we are. Let's show some pride on the court. Got it?"

Several of the players responded loudly, "Got it!"

Everyone huddled in a half circle around Coach.

"We're not all about offense," he reminded them. "Defense is the key. Keep your arms out, keep your feet moving." He spread his arms and bent his knees. "Pass the ball around, keep passing until you're open—then shoot. Don't be scared to shoot if you're open. But no wild shots. Get me?"

Coach looked at Ryan, then jabbed a finger in his direction. "Look for Ryan under the basket. He's tall, and he's strong." He spanked the clipboard against his leg. "Don't foul, go for the ball if it's loose, don't give up—never!"

He scanned his players. "You're the best I've ever coached. Win or lose, be proud!"

The players cheered and beat their chests. Jordan kissed his bicep a second time.

Coach announced the starting lineup. As Jordan expected, he was not in it. Then, with Ryan leading the way, the team ran into the gym and were greeted by the newly formed pep band.

"Sierra," he yelled as he passed her. He waved at Antonio.

"Get 'em, bro, "Antonio yelled. "Show 'em what you got."

Sierra, her glockenspiel in her arms, yelled, "Don't get hurt." She kissed her palm and then flung that kiss at him.

Jordan had read stories about hearts fluttering from love and characters who drew strength from the memory of a kiss. Now he knew that those stories were true.

Jordan had watched from the sidelines, gripping the seat of his chair when his team ran up the court toward their basket. Sweat filled his palms, sweat rolled down his face and dripped from his armpits, though he had yet to play any minutes. He looked up at the clock—time was chipping away. Their team was behind 13–9, with six minutes left in the first half.

We're close, he thought. When Ryan scored a three-point shot, Jordan stood up and yelled, "Dude! Dude!"

Ryan raised a triumphant fist at the crowd as he hurried back on defense.

Then their opponents scored, then *their* team scored again. It was back and forth, with a separation of only a few points.

Jordan wiped his face and looked at sweat gleaming on his forearm. *Man*, he thought, *I'm sweating just sitting here.* He drank from his water bottle, drank deeply.

When the buzzer sounded for halftime, he jogged to the locker room, where Coach, with a clipboard in his hand, paced up and down.

"We got this," he told the players. "Try not to foul! Don't shoot stupid. Box out. Keep your hands up, arms out." He pumped up the team, saying that they were only two points behind. He looked with a fiery stare at each player. For a second, Coach's eyes locked onto Jordan's eyes, then scanned his players one more time.

"Who are we?" Coach yelled.

"THE PATRIOTS!" they roared.

"Remember that!" He slapped the clipboard against his thigh and shouted, "Let's go!"

Then, with the starters first, the team hustled back into the gym.

To keep himself ready to play, Jordan stretched, jumped up and down, and did some jumping jacks. Then he sat down, heart racing, sweat once again filling his palms and armpits. He was proud to be on the team.

Finally, in the middle of the third quarter, Coach put him in.

He'd scored two baskets within a few minutes off the bench. When he sat down for breakfast the next morning, his dad handed him a newspaper. One effort, captured by the same photographer that had come to his school, involved Jordan leaping into the air—flying, his dad said—then releasing the ball just out of reach of a defender's hand. The photo was featured in the sports section, under the title "Good Samaritan, Good Hoops."

The accompanying story described Jordan Mendoza,

a seventh grader who had found a bag of documents and cash and returned it to its rightful owner, Mrs. Rosa Rodriguez, an elderly widow. This same seventh grader, noted the sportswriter, then contributed to a Patriots win over the previous champions, the Bears. Jordan's Patriots were now the city's reigning champs! The reporter closed the article by declaring that even George Washington, the school's namesake and father of this country, would have been proud.

Jordan grimaced at the photo. His tongue was sticking out again.

"Aaaaah," Jordan complained in horror. "Look at me—I look weird."

"My son look weird? *Imposible.* You have my genes." Mr. Mendoza turned to his wife and corrected himself. "I mean, Mom's genes." He giggled and stretched out his arms for a hug.

"You big flirt," Mrs. Mendoza cooed, accepting his embrace.

Jordan's dad went out and bought several more copies of the newspaper and stored them in a cardboard box. It was a Mendoza family memory worth saving.

34

JORDAN AND SIERRA met at the canal to say their goodbyes. The sky was gray, the sun eclipsed behind a bank of low-lying clouds. Wind rustled the trees and somewhere nearby a dog was barking.

Jordan had never felt so tender toward another person. He hurt. He didn't want Sierra to go. They stood facing each other.

"Do you really know me?" Sierra asked.

Jordan hesitated. He answered, "Yeah, I know you."

"Are you sure?" She bit her lower lip, then asked, "Are you sure you really like me?"

This was an easy answer. He took her hand in his. "You're nice."

"What else?" Sierra asked playfully.

"Kind."

"I don't know how you know that, but OK. What else?"

"I know that you're smarter than me."

Sierra giggled with a hand over her mouth, and said, "Like, duh!"

Jordan was dizzy with love. He almost danced in a circle, for he was crazy happy, but he couldn't take his eyes off her. Her hair was so shiny, her eyes filled with light.

They stood facing each other, only inches away. Then the inches closed, and they embraced. Sierra planted a kiss on his neck and grasped his once-injured hand.

"Does it still hurt? she asked.

My hand or my heart? Jordan wondered. "A little," he answered.

"I'll miss you," Sierra said.

"I'll miss you even more," Jordan responded.

They promised to text and call one another. They would keep in touch. They wouldn't forget their special feelings. Jordan promised to dream about her. And he did, once. In the dream, Sierra was walking down a busy street eating an ice cream cone. Jordan couldn't figure out what that meant.

After two months, the texts and calls came to an end. To keep Sierra from his thoughts, he no longer looked at her Instagram. TikTok? Not that either. Snapchat? He abandoned social media altogether. He became addicted to a video game called *StarHunt*. It was about a boy his age searching the universe for wicked space aliens.

On a Saturday morning in mid-February, Jordan sat on the sand near the canal. Although the air was cool and breezy, a few early cherry trees were blooming upstream. The three puppies were now frisky troublemakers. They barked at birds, then turned their heads to follow the birds' flights skyward. He let them off their leashes. Free, they rolled in and pawed at the sand, poking their noses into their cavernous creations. Each scrap of litter that they pulled up from the weeds was fascinating to them.

"Put that down," scolded Jordan.

Frances was carrying an egg carton in her jaws. The pup did as she was told, then bucked like a horse and raced to jump on Benny, who toppled over. The two started wrestling. Dawn, still the littlest, came running to join the fracas.

Jordan couldn't really be sure what thoughts dwelled in the folds of their tiny brains. He had to laugh, though. Not for the first time, he remembered his biology teacher telling the class that humans lived by five senses—taste, smell, sight, hearing, and touch. Did dogs do the same? He thought so.

That's what humans live *by*, he thought, but he guessed that they live *on* something else. Was it love? It sure had been a sad day when he and Sierra had said goodbye.

Now he sat watching the puppies playing on the beach. He wanted to tell them, "This is where I found you." But would they understand? *I hardly understand it myself*, he realized. He scooped up some sand and let it pour from his hand like an hourglass. That was what love was—time slipping away until eventually you forgot.

At that moment a girl his own age appeared on the bank, holding a plastic trash bag in her gloved hand. She stopped some distance from Jordan, until Benny untangled himself from the other two puppies and galloped toward her.

"Hey, you," she said to the puppy. "You're a cutie."

Benny barked at the girl.

"Benny!" Jordan commanded. "Stop that!" He rose to his feet, spanking sand from the back of his pants.

Benny barked at Jordan, then rejoined his two sisters. The three immediately began to wrestle again.

"They're so cute," said the girl. "So full of energy."

"They're full of energy all right," Jordan said, pretending to grumble, "but I don't know about the cute part."

"Oh yes they are!" the girl yelled with joy. "They're super cute."

Jordan shrugged and tried to keep from smiling.

They stood in silence, watching the puppies and, at the same time, trying to observe each other.

When the girl took a few steps toward him, Jordan didn't know what else to say except "Hi."

"Hi," the girl said. She was as tall as him, with long hair the color of the sand at their feet. "I was supposed to go on a litter patrol," she added, looking over her shoulder at the bushes from which she had emerged. "But I guess I had the wrong date. It must be tomorrow."

Jordan smiled. "I get dates wrong all the time."

"All the time?"

"Yeah, well, most of the time."

Out of the corner of his eye, Jordan noticed that all three pups were now struggling over the egg carton. But he couldn't be bothered with them right now. Someone new and interesting was standing in front of him, a girl with pierced ears, a bright smile, freckles on her cheeks, a leaf in her hair, jeans torn at the knees. *No, interesting is the wrong word*, he told himself. She was the most beautiful girl he had ever seen.

She put her plastic bag down and peeled off her gloves. She sat down on the sand, cross-legged, an invitation for Jordan to sit down too. They watched the water flowing downstream, carrying little rafts of fallen petals from the flowering trees.

Who is this girl? he wondered. His heart was pounding and he couldn't think of anything to say. And then, dropping his head like a pony, he asked, "What's your name?"

She looked down, suddenly shy as well. Then she smiled and answered, "Dawn."

"Dawn," he repeated, in a near whisper. What were the chances? He liked that name, liked it lot. He could picture it inked on his bicep, expanding whenever he flexed his growing muscles.

"What's yours?" she asked.

"Jordan."

"Jordan?" she repeated, pouring sand absently between her fingers. "That's a nice name."

An unexpected gust of wind whistled through the trees, sending a flurry of white petals into the air, like snow. Shouting with happiness, Dawn and Jordan thrust their hands upward to catch them.